A PLACE TO CALL HOME
BOOK TWO

BRIGHT ARE THE STARS

AL & JOANNA LACY

Multnomah® Publishers *Sisters, Oregon*

BRIGHT ARE THE STARS
© 2006 by ALJO PRODUCTIONS, INC.
published by Multnomah Publishers, Inc.

International Standard Book Number: 1-59052-563-9

Cover image of man byLois Ellen Frank/Corbis
Cover image of tepees by Jay F. Koelzer/Index Stock Imagery

Printed in the United States of America
Multnomah is a trademark of Multnomah Publishers, Inc.,
and is registered in the U.S. Patent and Trademark Office.
The colophon is a trademark of Multnomah Publishers, Inc.

For information:
Multnomah Publishers, Inc., 601 North Larch Street, Sisters, Oregon 97759

Library of Congress Cataloging-in-Publication Data

Lacy, Al.
  Bright are the stars / Al and JoAnna Lacy.
    p. cm. — (A place to call home ; bk. 2)
  ISBN 1-59052-563-9
  1. Cherokee Indians—Fiction. 2. Indian Territory—Fiction. I. Lacy, JoAnna.
II. Title.
PS3562.A256B75 2006
813'.54—dc22

2006018147

06 07 08 09 10 11 12 — 10 9 8 7 6 5 4 3 2 1 0

With deep affection, we dedicate this book to our precious friend
Betty Dupps, who has recently gone through her own dark valley.
But our loving Lord has revealed to her in, through,
and by His all-sufficient grace that "bright are the stars."
God bless you, dear one.
Al and JoAnna

1 PETER 1:2

preface

n the sixteenth century, the Cherokee Indians occupied mountain areas of North Carolina, Georgia, Alabama, and Tennessee. They had a settled, advanced agrarian culture. In 1540, they were visited by the Hernando De Soto expedition, and the Spanish explorer later reported that he was impressed with the Cherokee people.

In 1820, the Cherokees adopted a republican form of government, and in 1827 they established themselves as the Cherokee Nation.

By 1832, much pressure was being put on the government in Washington DC to remove the Indians elsewhere so the white people could have their land. This, coupled with Andrew Jackson (who was known to be prejudiced against Indians) being president of the United States at the time, spelled doom for the Cherokees as the pressure mounted for the removal of all Indians to the West. There were five tribes known as the Civilized Tribes: the Cherokee, the Chickasaw, the Choctaw, the Creek, and the Seminole. These five tribes were slated to occupy the land in the West known as Indian Territory.

The Cherokee Nation's leading chief, John Ross, a mixed-blood Cherokee, struggled hard against President Jackson's administration to keep his people from being put off their land.

Ross's struggle continued when Martin Van Buren became president in 1837. The opposition was too great, however, and as the story was told in the first book of this trilogy, *Cherokee Rose*, in the winter of 1838–39, some fifteen thousand North Carolina Cherokees were forced by the U.S. Army to make the one-thousand-mile journey westward to Indian Territory, which is now the state of Oklahoma. This harrowing journey, during which over four thousand Cherokees died, has become known as the Trail of Tears.

The Cherokees of Georgia, Alabama, and Tennessee had already been forced to go to Indian Territory, also having lost their homes. The same thing was happening to the people of the other four Civilized Tribes.

Repeatedly forced to surrender their lands, the people of the Cherokee Nation, as well as those of the other four tribes, were hoping to find in Indian Territory "a place to call home."

prologue

wo outstanding Cherokee chiefs lived during the period of history covered in the first book of this trilogy, *Cherokee Rose*, and a portion of what is covered in this book. Their names are still revered today by the Cherokee Indians: Chief John Ross and Chief Sequoyah.

John Ross was born October 3, 1790, near Lookout Mountain in the Smoky Mountains of North Carolina. Born of a Scottish father and a mother who was part Cherokee, the blue-eyed, fair-skinned John Ross (whose Cherokee name was Tsan-Usdi) grew up as an Indian. Courageous and highly intelligent, Ross became the leader of the Cherokee resistance to the white man's planned acquisition of land the Cherokees had lived on for centuries. Because of Ross's valor in fighting for his people, he was made a Cherokee chief at the young age of twenty-two. Since he was mostly white, though in his heart he was all Cherokee, the chiefs of every Cherokee village in the Smoky Mountains voted to honor him with a second name: Chief White Bird. He married a full-blooded Cherokee woman named Quatie and in 1819 was voted in as president of the National Council of Cherokees.

With the threat of the Indians' forced move to the West hanging over their heads, John Ross put up a spirited defense for his people. His petitions to President Andrew Jackson, under whom he had fought in the Creek War (1813–14), went unheeded. On May 28, 1830, the U.S. Congress, following Jackson's leadership, established the Indian Removal Act.

In 1838–39, when Martin Van Buren was president, Ross had no choice but to lead his people, under duress from soldiers of the U.S. Army, toward an unknown western prairie called Indian Territory. On the journey, his wife, Quatie, took sick and died.

Sequoyah was born c. 1773 in North Carolina, and was called Sogwali by his parents. After both parents died while he was yet a youth, some Bible-preaching missionaries to the Cherokee people named him Sequoyah.

Having been a Cherokee chief for some five years, in 1809 Sequoyah began working to develop a system of writing for his people, believing that increased knowledge would help the Cherokee Nation maintain their independence from the whites. By 1821 he had developed a system of eighty-six symbols that made up the Cherokee alphabet. The simplicity of his system enabled students to learn it rapidly, and soon Cherokees throughout their nation were teaching it in their schools and publishing books and newspapers in their own language, printing them on their own presses.

Chief Sequoyah had a great interest in the Bible, which was introduced to him in English by the same missionaries who renamed him, and by 1823 he had translated the entire Bible into the Cherokee language, and thousands of copies were printed.

In 1825, the General Council of the Cherokee Nation presented Sequoyah a silver medal for these accomplishments.

introduction

s told in the first volume of this trilogy, *Cherokee Rose*, on Monday morning, October 17, 1838, General Winfield Scott of the United States Army arrived in Cherokee territory of the Smoky Mountains of North Carolina with seven thousand soldiers to prepare the Indians for the journey.

Among the fifteen thousand Cherokees in the Smoky Mountains was a chief named Bando. Chief Bando, his wife, Nevarra, and their family had come to know the Lord Jesus Christ as Saviour under the ministry of missionary Layne Ward and his wife, Sylvia. In the family were their daughters, Tarbee and Naya, their son-in-law, Walugo (Naya's husband), and their granddaughter, eighteen-year-old Cherokee Rose, who was half-Cherokee, half-white. Naya, who was white, had been adopted by Bando and Nevarra when she was a baby.

During the long, tedious journey westward, the Cherokees found that many of the soldiers hated Indians and were brutal toward them.

However, one young soldier, Lieutenant Britt Claiborne, did his best to protect the Indians from the brutal soldiers. His kindness toward the Cherokees soon drew the attention of Cherokee Rose. Britt and Cherokee Rose became acquainted, and she soon learned that twenty-one-year-old Britt was a Christian and that he was a quarter Cherokee.

As the journey progressed, Britt and Cherokee Rose fell in love. Knowing they would have to part once the Cherokees arrived in Indian Territory, they began to pray for a miracle from God that would allow them to stay together and become husband and wife.

During the long journey, some 4,239 Cherokees died and were buried, including Cherokee Rose's mother, Naya.

In late March 1839, the surviving ten thousand-plus Cherokees arrived at Fort Gibson in Indian Territory, escorted by General Winfield Scott and his troops.

The North Carolina Cherokees were gathered in an open field near the fort, and a government official explained that the other four Civilized Tribes and the Cherokees who had come earlier from Tennessee, Georgia, and Alabama were already situated in the Territory and were happy in their new home.

General Winfield Scott then turned the North Carolina Cherokees over to Fort Gibson's commandant, General Austin Danford. Scott announced to his men that they would be heading back eastward later that day. He then had a private talk with Britt

Claiborne and told him that since he was a quarter Cherokee, he was eligible to serve on the Cherokee Police Force in the Territory. If Britt would apply for the job at the Cherokee General Council headquarters, Scott was sure he would be hired.

Britt jumped on his horse, rode to Tahlequah, the new Cherokee national capital eighteen miles northeast of the fort, and applied for the job. Because of his military background, he was quickly hired. When he arrived back at the fort, General Scott told him he would see that he received an honorable discharge from the army.

Britt went to Cherokee Rose and told her what had happened. Together, they praised the Lord for this answer to prayer. God had given them their miracle. Cherokee Rose asked Britt if he would go to her father and get his permission to marry her. She was surprised when Britt told her he had done that on his way back from the office of the Cherokee General Council, and Walugo had happily given his permission.

General Austin Danford had told the North Carolina Cherokees that they would be taken to an area many miles southwest of the fort the next day. Each family would be assigned a large section of land, and they would soon be given wood to build their cabins.

The next morning, a large number of mounted soldiers under the command of Captain Lawrence Kirkland led the North Carolina Cherokees southwestward across Indian Territory. The Cherokees were pleased to see the rolling, grassy prairie, the great stands of trees, the many streams, and the fertile farmland. They saw that many of the Indians who were already settled there had large herds of cattle in fenced pastures.

By midafternoon on that Wednesday, March 27, the soldiers led the Indians onto the land that would be theirs. They were glad to see that it was like all the other land they had seen that day.

They set up camp, and Britt Claiborne pitched his tent next to Walugo's wagon. All over the massive area there was laughter around the campfires, something that had not been heard among the North Carolina Cherokees since they had been forced from their homes in the Smoky Mountains. Families chatted together, talking about the cabins and farms that would be theirs.

Britt and Cherokee Rose sat together next to a small fire and held hands. "I don't know about you," Britt said, "but to me, Indian Territory is already feeling a lot like home."

Cherokee Rose lifted a hand and stroked his cheek. "I didn't think it would happen so quickly for me, but I really have found a place to call home."

Let us begin, now, with the story of the North Carolina Cherokees as they settle in their new home in Indian Territory.

ritt Claiborne rode northeastward in Indian Territory across
the rolling prairie in the brilliant morning sunlight. He had just left the
area where the North Carolina Cherokees
had been given land for their farms and was
headed toward the Cherokee General Council
headquarters in Tahlequah, the Cherokee national capital. There he would be given two
new uniforms so he could begin his work as
a police officer on the Indian Territory Police
Force.

Trotting his big black gelding, Blackie, across the uneven land, Britt looked back over his shoulder and smiled as he ran his gaze over the many circles of wagons and the numerous tents pitched among them. He felt a deep satisfaction in his heart, knowing that the North Carolina Cherokees would soon have their own cabins and could begin their lives anew. Though they still felt the loss of their loved ones and friends on the long journey to Indian Territory, there was much happiness in their hearts. They were finally settled on their own land.

Britt rode into a heavily wooded area where the trees were beginning to bud, and his thoughts went to Cherokee Rose, who would soon become his wife. "Thank You, Lord," he said, "for bringing that wonderful young lady into my life. I love her so much."

Suddenly, Britt stiffened as he saw three grim-faced men on horseback in U.S. Army uniforms ride out of a dense section of cottonwood trees a few yards ahead. Their eyes were fixed on his, and their rifles were pointed directly at him.

He recognized them, and a shudder pulsed through him. On the long journey from North Carolina, Britt had seen a number of his fellow soldiers brutally mistreat the Indians, and often he had been forced to confront those soldiers to protect the Indians from harm. He knew that many of the soldiers held a grudge against him. Now he was facing three of the most hateful ones.

With his heart pounding, Britt wondered what they were doing in Indian Territory. They were supposed to be on their way to a fort back East.

Britt drew up and pulled rein, his heart still pounding, and ran his gaze from face to face. "What are you men doing here in Indian Territory?"

The one in the middle scowled. "We've come back here to get

even with you. You're gonna pay for what you did to us."

Before Britt could say another word, all three rifles roared. He felt the bullets rip into his upper body, and blood spattered his jacket. As he was falling from the saddle, he suddenly found himself gasping and sitting up in his bedroll on the ground under the moon and stars. He felt a drop of perspiration grow cold on his brow and trickle down his face.

He was conscious that his racing heartbeat was beginning to slow as his head cleared. He raised his eyes toward the starry heavens and said, "Thank You, Lord, that it was only a bad dream."

He ran his gaze to the covered wagon a few feet away, and he could hear Cherokee Rose's soft, even breathing inside. He glanced beneath the wagon and could see her father's bedroll on the other side. Walugo was fast asleep.

Wide awake now, Britt decided to take a brief walk and settle his nerves before trying to go back to sleep. He slipped out of the bedroll and headed toward a small stream nearby to get a drink. He glanced around at the wagons, tents, and men sleeping outside in bedrolls and noticed three wagons with pale lamplight glowing behind the canvas covers.

Must be some others who are having trouble sleeping.

Walking as quietly as possible, Britt passed one dimly lit wagon and heard a mother softly singing an Indian lullaby to a fussy baby. He stopped and listened for a moment. Soon the infant's fussing stopped, and the singing ceased. Britt smiled to himself as the lantern light was extinguished and all was quiet again inside the wagon.

Britt looked toward heaven and silently thanked his heavenly Father for bringing the North Carolina Cherokees to this fertile territory where they could farm their land and know peace and contentment.

Moments later, as he drew near the stream, he saw a lone figure seated on a log next to the gurgling water. He recognized sixty-six-year-old Chief Sequoyah, his silver hair highlighted by the moon and stars.

Sequoyah rose to his feet, smiling. "You are having a problem getting to sleep too, my friend?"

"I have been asleep," Britt said, "but I woke up and decided to come to the stream to get a drink."

Britt knelt on the bank of the stream and drank. When he rose to his feet, the chief was seated on the log once again. He patted the space beside him and said, "If you are in no hurry to return to your bedroll, please sit down."

"No hurry," Britt said and sat down. "So you were having a problem getting to sleep?"

Sequoyah nodded. "Nothing bad anymore. I just have so much on my mind. I keep thinking of that long, horrible journey with so many of my Cherokee people dying." He drew a deep breath and let it out. "It is so good to finally have a place to call home, to see my people already showing signs of happiness. Something I have not seen in such a long time. The joy of it keeps me awake." Sequoyah thumbed tears from his eyes and looked at Britt. "It is so good."

"I can already see a change in your countenance," Britt said. "I know you love your people with all your heart."

The silver-haired chief looked up at the night sky and sighed. "The stars are bright tonight, aren't they?"

Britt scanned the starry heavens for a long moment, then nodded and met Sequoyah's gaze. "They sure are, Chief."

"I believe the stars are so bright because the North Carolina Cherokees are already finding happiness in their new home."

Britt nodded. "I'm sure you're right."

Sequoyah let a smile spread from ear to ear. "I am glad you

agree. It makes me feel better, knowing it is not just this old man's feeling. Well, my friend," the chief said as he stood, "now I know I can get to sleep."

The two men headed back toward the camp and told each other good night as they parted company. Britt passed the covered wagon where he had heard the mother singing to her fussy baby earlier and noted the lantern glow inside and heard the mother singing to the baby again.

When he entered the circle where Walugo's wagon was located, he saw that Walugo was still sound asleep in his bedroll, but movement at the canvas opening at the rear of the wagon caught his eye. He moved up close and whispered, "Sweetheart, what are you doing awake?"

Cherokee Rose was on her knees, holding on to the tailgate with one hand. "I…I just happened to wake up a few minutes ago and found myself thirsty. I got a drink from the water jug, then decided I would just take a peek at you in your bedroll. When I looked your direction, I could see that your bedroll was empty. I wondered where you might have gone."

Britt stepped up closer, kissed the hand that held the tailgate, and said, "I woke up and was thirsty, too, so I took a little walk to the stream. Chief Sequoyah was there, and he and I chatted for a little while. I'm going to get some sleep now, and I want you to do the same."

She smiled. "All right, *boss*."

He kissed the hand again. "See you in the morning. I love you."

"I love you, too."

As Britt walked toward his bedroll, he whispered back over his shoulder, "But I will love you even more by sunrise. My love for you grows day and night."

Cherokee Rose felt the warmth of his love in her heart and said, "Bless him, Lord. Thank You for giving me such a wonderful man. I will be so glad when I am Mrs. Britt Claiborne."

The sun rose into a clear azure sky the next morning, March 28, 1839. As the North Carolina Cherokees left their beds and made ready to begin the new day, there was a great measure of happiness in their hearts as the men built cook-fires, the women began preparing breakfast, and the children played together and laughed gaily.

At Walugo's wagon, Britt Claiborne built a cook-fire while Cherokee Rose took food for breakfast from the wagon. They playfully argued about which one loved the other the most.

"Miss Cherokee Rose," Britt said, "my love for you grew so much last night that the Lord had to extend the edges of the universe so it wouldn't explode!"

She was about to come back with her reply when her father hopped out of the rear of the wagon with a bucket in his hand and said, "I hope you will always argue like this, even when you are married."

His daughter smiled. "I can guarantee you that we will, dear father. Even though it is I who love Britt the most, I want him to always argue with me about it."

Walugo laughed, lifted the bucket, and said, "I will go get some water from the stream."

Many Cherokees were at the stream getting water as Walugo drew up. He noticed Chief John Ross at one spot along the bank of the stream and stepped up beside him.

Ross smiled as he lifted his full bucket from the stream. "Go ahead, Walugo. There's plenty of water for everybody."

Walugo dipped his bucket into the gurgling stream and said, "I am glad the Lord supplied us with lots of water."

As they walked back toward the camp, Ross said, "I heard a rumor, Walugo. I heard that Britt has been hired as a police officer on the Indian Territory Police Force. Is it true?"

"It is true," Walugo said. "And there is more good news. Britt and my daughter have set their wedding date. It will be next month, April 28."

"They will make a perfect couple. It is obvious that the Lord made them for each other. They will have a wonderful marriage." As those words came from John's mouth, tears filled his eyes. "I…I sure do miss my Quatie."

Tears glistened in Walugo's eyes as he said, "I understand, John. I miss my Naya so very much."

Their pace slowed, and there was silence between the two men as they thought of the wives they had buried on the journey from North Carolina.

"Quatie and Naya would have been so happy here in this new home," Walugo said.

"Yes, they would," John said, "but this beautiful land is nothing compared to the glorious land where they are now."

Walugo nodded. "Oh, how true that is! It makes heaven so much sweeter, doesn't it?"

"Indeed it does. Indeed it does."

They picked up their pace once again, and as they walked, Walugo placed his hand on his friend's shoulder, and a smile passed between them.

After everyone in the camp had finished their breakfast, Chief John Ross sent some young men to hurry through the camp and announce a meeting of all Christian Cherokees in one hour, asking them to bring their Bibles.

At Walugo's wagon, word of the meeting came quickly, and as soon as the young messenger hurried on, Cherokee Rose's bright eyes were alive with excitement as she approached Britt and her father and said, "Now that Pastor Ward has agreed to perform the wedding, I must go and tell my grandparents and Aunt Tarbee and some of my closest friends that we have set the date. I will be back in plenty of time to attend the meeting, but I just *have* to go and share our good news! Is that all right with both of you?"

Walugo chuckled. "Of course it is all right, my dear. Go and tell the whole Cherokee Nation if you want to."

hief John Ross threaded his way through the crowd, speaking to people in a friendly manner. He spotted Pastor Jesse Bushyhead standing with a couple of men and made his way to them.

"Hello, John Ross," Pastor Bushyhead said. "My friends and I were just discussing what this meeting might be about."

John shook hands with all three, then looked at the Bibles they were carrying. "I see each of you has a Bible in the Cherokee language. I know you can read and speak English well, but I am glad you use the Bible Chief Sequoyah gave us in our language."

"We still know our Cherokee language better than we know English," Pastor Bushyhead said. "We thank the Lord every day for putting it on Chief Sequoyah's heart to translate God's Word into our language."

Ross leaned close to them and said in a low voice so others around them could not hear, "That is what this meeting is about—Chief Sequoyah's labor of love in translating God's Word into the Cherokee language. I feel that we all must express our appreciation to him."

Pastor Bushyhead patted Ross's arm. "What you are doing is very good. May God bless you for it."

John Ross gave him a warm smile, then pressed on through the crowd. He saw Chief Sequoyah just ahead talking with a small group of men and women. He stepped up to Sequoyah and said, "Please forgive me for interrupting your conversation, Chief, but I want you to stay close to the front of the crowd when I am speaking."

Sequoyah frowned. "Why, my friend?"

"You will find out shortly. Just stay close, all right?"

"At your request, I will do that."

As Ross continued to press through the crowd, he came upon Layne and Sylvia Ward.

"Are you ready as we planned?" Ross asked.

"Sure am," Layne said.

"Good. I want you and Mrs. Ward to take a place near the front of the crowd."

Sylvia smiled and squeezed her husband's hand. "I'm so eager to see the look on Chief Sequoyah's face when you call him up to stand before the crowd."

"It won't be long now," Ross said.

Within less than a minute, nearly every eye in the crowd was fixed on Chief John Ross as he stood before them and called out, "All right, everybody! Gather around and sit down on the ground!"

When everyone was finally settled, John Ross lifted his voice so all could hear and said, "I very much appreciate every one of you coming to this meeting, especially when you did not know what it was about. I know you will be glad you came when you find out."

Ross then pointed toward the Wards and asked them to stand up.

"All of you are acquainted with Layne and Sylvia Ward. I want to remind you that this couple has carried out their wonderful ministry among us North Carolina Cherokees for many years. A great number of you have come to know Jesus Christ as your Saviour through their work."

Hands were being waved, many amens were heard, and some called out the names of the missionaries, telling them they loved them.

Layne and Sylvia were both wiping tears from their eyes as John Ross went on.

"As all of you know, this unselfish couple came all the way from North Carolina with us because they love us, and they want to continue serving the Lord among us. You also know that Pastor Okluskie, who died from pneumonia on the journey from North Carolina, was pastor of the church in Chief Bando's village, where my membership is. We have asked Layne to become our pastor. After much prayer, he has accepted the offer. Layne Ward is now pastor of our church!"

When the cheering subsided, John Ross announced that beginning next Sunday, each of the North Carolina Cherokee churches would find their own spot on the surrounding prairie to begin holding their services. He said that their pastors had already met about this and would contact their members to let them know where they would meet.

With his Bible in hand, Ross set his eyes on Chief Sequoyah, who as promised, was sitting close by, and said so that all could hear, "Chief Sequoyah, I would like to have you come and stand beside me."

Pleased puzzlement showed on Sequoyah's wrinkled face as he rose to his feet and stepped up beside Ross, facing the crowd.

Ross then looked down at Layne Ward and said, "Pastor, would you come and stand on my other side, please?"

After Layne had done so, John Ross ran his gaze over the captivated crowd and said, "Friends, I see that most of you have your Bibles. Please turn to Psalm 68."

While the sound of fluttering pages flowed softly in the air, John Ross looked at Layne and said, "All right, Pastor, you read the verse that we discussed, then I will take it from there."

When the sound of fluttering pages faded into silence, Pastor Ward said, "All right, friends, I want you to fix your attention here in Psalm 68 on verse eleven. I will read that to you first in the Cherokee language, then I will read it in English."

Speaking loud and clear, Pastor Ward read the verse first in Cherokee, then in English: "The Lord gave the word: great was the company of those that published it."

John Ross laid an affectionate hand on the shoulder of Chief Sequoyah and spoke to the crowd. "We all owe the fact that we have God's Word in the Cherokee language to this dear man. Yes, God in heaven gave the Word, but He chose to have true believers on earth publish it. Our Cherokee printing presses have printed and published the Bible in our language, but had Chief Sequoyah not given us our alphabet and translated God's Word into our language, we would have no Bible to publish."

Everyone in the crowd stood up and applauded and cheered their beloved Chief Sequoyah, who wiped tears from his cheeks.

When the applause and the cheering subsided, Sequoyah ran his eyes over their faces and said with a quavering voice, "Thank you. I—I cannot put into words what a blessing it is to me to see so many Cherokee people carrying a Bible and to know that they believe it."

Bibles were lifted high and waved by the people as they once again cheered for Chief Sequoyah. When the Bible waving and cheering abated, Chief Sequoyah returned to his place in the crowd.

Ross then looked at Britt Claiborne and Cherokee Rose where they sat on the ground and asked them to come to the front and stand with him.

Cherokee Rose looked at Britt questioningly. He shrugged his shoulders, then stood up, took her hand, and helped her to her feet.

John Ross smiled at them as they approached him, then said, "Please turn around and face the crowd."

The Cherokees looked at the couple admiringly. Everyone knew that Cherokee Rose's mother was white, but they also knew that the young woman who stood before them was a full-blooded Cherokee in her heart.

Having watched Lieutenant Britt Claiborne protect so many of them from the white soldiers on the long journey westward, the crowd felt confident that in Britt's heart, he also was a full-blooded Cherokee.

As Britt gazed out at the large number of people, a new determination took hold of him. *Lord*, he said in his heart, *You helped me to protect many of these dear people on the long journey to this new land. Please help in my new job as a police officer here in Indian Territory. Give me wisdom like You gave to King Solomon as I do my part to care for them.*

John Ross said to the crowd, "I know that many of you have been hearing rumors that my friend Britt Claiborne is no longer a lieutenant in the United States Army, but has been hired as a police officer on the Indian Territory Police Force. Well, I talked to Cherokee Rose's father, Walugo, just after sunrise this morning, and he confirmed that those rumors are indeed true."

The crowd applauded and cheered, and Britt gave them a friendly wave. Moments later, when he knew he could be heard, he said, "Please pray for me. I want to do the best job possible when I begin my new career as a police officer here in Indian Territory."

Chief John Ross glanced at Britt and Cherokee Rose, then said to the crowd, "My friend Walugo also confirmed something else to me this morning. This fine young couple have set their wedding date. They are going to be married on Sunday afternoon, April 28…a month from today. Pastor Ward has happily consented to perform the ceremony."

The Indians lifted up a rousing ovation, and the smiling couple held hands and waved at them.

Ross let the ovation diminish, then said, "It has been so long since I have seen my Cherokee people this happy. It is good to see that you are already enjoying your new home so much."

Ross then looked at Pastor Jesse Bushyhead, who was nearby, and asked him to come to the front and close the meeting in prayer.

Just before John Ross bowed his head for Pastor Bushyhead's prayer, he noticed five riders sitting on their horses several yards to the rear of the crowd looking on. Ross knew they were Cherokees by how they were dressed, but they were not North Carolina Cherokees. He wondered how long they had been looking on, and why they were there.

The five Cherokee riders were watching the crowd disperse when they saw John Ross walking toward them. As he drew up, they smiled at him, and the oldest of the five said, "Chief John Ross, we are Tennessee Cherokees, and I am Chief Vandigo." Then he introduced the others as Pidini and Armido, who were brothers, and Jocko, and Serindan. "We just learned that the North Carolina Cherokees had arrived, and we have come to welcome you to Indian Territory."

"That is very kind of you, Chief Vandigo," Ross said. "I…ah… noticed that you called me by name."

Vandigo nodded. "I have seen you each time you held meetings for the chiefs of all the Cherokees in the South."

Ross smiled. "Oh, I see."

"When my four companions and I asked some of the North Carolina Cherokees where we might find Chief John Ross, we were especially pleased to be told that a Christian meeting was in progress, over which you were presiding."

"Were you pleased because you men are Christians yourselves?"

"Yes, born again and washed in the blood of the Lamb of God. Missionaries to the Tennessee Cherokees led us to Jesus."

"Wonderful!" Ross said.

"We would also like to meet Chief Sequoyah," Vandigo said, "and express our gratitude to him that we now have the Bible in our language."

"Follow me. I am sure Chief Sequoyah is still here."

As the Tennessee Cherokees rode their horses and followed Chief John Ross, he called the people together again. He had some men he wanted them to meet.

Soon there was a big crowd once more.

John Ross explained that the five strangers beside him were Tennessee Cherokees and they were Christians. He introduced them by name, then told the crowd that Chief Vandigo wanted to speak to them.

Just before Ross stepped aside, he pointed out a silver-haired man close by and whispered to Vandigo that he was Chief Sequoyah.

Chief Vandigo warmly welcomed them all to Indian Territory. Then he looked at the silver-haired man and said, "Chief Sequoyah, would you please come and stand here with me?"

When Sequoyah stepped up to him, Chief Vandigo said, "My dear brother in Christ, I speak for all the Tennessee Cherokees when I say thank you for giving the Cherokee people the Bible in their own language."

Once again, there was much cheering from the crowd for Chief Sequoyah, who was noticeably embarrassed.

Three

arly on the following Saturday morning, Britt Claiborne was eating breakfast with Cherokee Rose and her father. After breakfast, Britt planned to leave for Tahlequah, where he would pick up the uniforms that had been made for him.

The fragrant aroma of coffee permeated the air as a cool breeze wafted through the camp, stirring the cook-fires. Cherokee Rose had prepared a breakfast of bacon and flap-jacks.

As the three of them were eating the simple fare, Cherokee Rose sighed, looked at Britt, and said, "I will be so happy when we are married and have our cabin and a good cookstove. It's hard to prepare anything very tasty over these outdoor fires."

Britt grinned at her. "Now, sweetheart, I'm sure your father will agree that you do just fine cooking outdoors over a fire."

"That is right," Walugo said. "You do a beautiful job cooking like this. But from what the soldiers tell us, it won't be long before you have an indoor kitchen again, less than a month now."

"Yes!" she said. "Less than a month!"

"I'm glad the soldiers are going to help us with the construction," Britt said, "or it would be a lot longer." He leaned over and kissed Cherokee Rose's forehead. "Before you know it, we'll be married, and you'll be cooking all our meals in our own homey kitchen."

Walugo cleared his throat. "I...ah...sure hope I will get to eat some of your cooking after you marry this fortunate young man, daughter."

Cherokee Rose laughed. "Oh, you most certainly *will*, Father."

When breakfast was over, Walugo and Cherokee Rose walked with Britt to a nearby tree, where his saddled horse, Blackie, was tied.

She looked at Britt and said, "You have always looked handsome in your army uniform, but I am sure you will look even more handsome in a police uniform."

Britt hugged her and kissed her cheek. "Flatterer. I'm just glad that I will soon be the husband of the most beautiful woman in the world."

"Now who is being the flatterer?" she said.

Britt swung into the saddle, and father and daughter waved to him as he rode away.

Walugo then left the wagon to spend some time with other

Cherokee men to plan the plowing and seeding they would soon be doing on their farms since spring had come.

An idea had been forming in Cherokee Rose's mind since she and Britt set the date for their wedding. She made quick work of washing and drying the breakfast dishes, then walked briskly toward the wagon belonging to Pastor Layne Ward and Sylvia.

As Britt Claiborne rode his big black gelding northeastward across the rolling prairie, he looked back over his shoulder and ran his gaze over the many circles of wagons and the tents scattered among them. In his mind, he pictured the log cabins that shortly would dot the land.

Soon Blackie carried his master toward the familiar wooded area ahead, and a chill slithered down Britt's spine. He pulled rein, stunned by the shock that came over him as he recalled the bad dream he had experienced a couple of nights before.

Blackie skidded to a halt, and Britt vividly recalled the sensation of the bullets ripping into his body in the nightmare. "Thank You, Lord," he said. "Thank You that it was only a bad dream."

The horror that had overtaken him so suddenly faded away, and Britt put his horse to a fast trot, heading toward Tahlequah.

"Well, hello, Cherokee Rose. This is a nice surprise!"

Sylvia laid down the broom she had been using to clean the inside of her wagon, climbed gingerly over the tailgate, and gave her friend a quick hug. Noting the serious look on Cherokee Rose's face, she said, "Honey, is something wrong? You look so sober."

A soft smile broke across the Indian maiden's face. "Oh, no. Nothing is wrong. I just need some very important advice."

"Well, honey, Pastor isn't here right now. Can you come back—"

"Oh, no, no. I need to talk to *you*, Sylvia. Is this a good time?"

"Why, of course. Let's sit down here close to the cook-fire. There's coffee in the coffeepot, still warm from breakfast. Want a cup? There's plenty left."

"Yes. That sounds good."

Sylvia reached inside the wagon for two cups and picked up the blackened coffeepot from the embers. She handed Cherokee Rose a cup, filled it for her, then filled one for herself.

"I don't know all the answers in this world," Sylvia said as they sat down on the worn wooden chairs near the fire, "but I'll do my best to help you."

Cherokee Rose said in a soft voice, "Sylvia, I want to be the best wife possible to Britt, and I thought since you are such a wonderful wife to your husband, you would be the perfect person to ask."

Sylvia smiled and touched fingertips to her forehead. "Honey, I…I'm glad you see me that way. I'll do my best to help you by showing you what God's Word says about it. Let's go inside the wagon."

Both women finished their coffee, then climbed in the rear of the wagon.

Sylvia asked Cherokee Rose to sit down on the bed, then took her Bible from a small table and sat beside her. As she began flipping pages, she said, "I want us to read a portion of Ephesians chapter 5 together. It speaks of the relationship the Lord wants between Christian husbands and wives."

"I have read the book of Ephesians many times, but I am sure I will see more with you leading me than I have seen before."

Sylvia smiled. "Read verses 22 through 33 to me."

Cherokee Rose set her eyes on the page and began to read aloud.

When she finished, Sylvia said, "All right, honey, let's take a good look at this. As I said, this passage speaks of the relationship the Lord wants between Christian husbands and wives and the responsibilities both have before God. In God's plan, the husband is to be the head of the wife as Christ is the head of the church. Christ's being the Saviour of the church should find an analogy in the Christian husband, who should be the same to his wife—her ever-vigilant and self-denying protector, guardian, and deliverer. The last verse in the passage says the husband should love his wife, and the wife should reverence her husband."

"This is good," Cherokee Rose said. "Do you have something I can write this down on?"

"Certainly." Sylvia went to a box at the front of the wagon and returned with paper, pen, and ink.

Cherokee Rose made notes on what Sylvia had already pointed out, then said, "I will have no problem reverencing Britt, I guarantee you."

"One more thing to remember in a successful Christian marriage, honey. Always, *always*, *ALWAYS*, put the Lord first. If both Britt and Cherokee Rose put God first, then you will please each other and know real happiness as you work as partners in this beautiful union called marriage. There is nothing sweeter or more gratifying as a wife than to know that your husband is happy and content with the home you are making for him. He then will do everything in his power to do the same for you. If you both follow God's plan as He has laid it out in His Word, then everybody wins."

Cherokee Rose sat quietly, absorbing Sylvia's words.

"Now, don't misunderstand me," Sylvia said. "I'm not saying that everything will be absolutely perfect in a marriage, even when the Lord is put first. Since the Bible says we are all sinners, this means, for one thing, that both the husband and the wife have their imperfections. There will naturally be some disagreements between you and Britt along the way. But when these times come, the two of you need to talk about it, pray together over it, and let the Lord help you resolve it according to His will."

Tears misted Cherokee Rose's dark eyes. "I saw this very thing in my parents' marriage, Sylvia. Father and Mother handled any differences they had exactly as you just described. They had a beautiful marriage. Thank you for taking the time to explain it all to me."

Sylvia took hold of Cherokee Rose's hand. "My dear, since your deep desire is to be the right kind of wife to Britt, and I am sure his deep desire is to be the right kind of husband to you, the Lord will bless your home in a wonderful way."

Both women rose to their feet.

"Thank you so much for your help," Cherokee Rose said.

Sylvia hugged her friend, then looked deeply into her eyes. "I know that you and Britt are going to have a very happy and wonderful marriage."

The sun was lowering toward the horizon when Britt Claiborne rode up to Walugo's wagon, where Cherokee Rose was preparing supper. She smiled when she saw him in the saddle, all decked out in a black uniform with a shiny silver badge on his chest.

He wore a black broad-brimmed hat, and on his waist was a pearl-handled Colt .45 revolver in a black leather holster and gun belt. She also saw a bolt-action rifle in a black leather case attached to the saddle.

A twinge of fear passed through her heart at the sight of the guns. Britt, of course, was a soldier and had handled guns, but the sight of the weapons gave her a cold chill. *He is a lawman now, and you must support him in what the Lord has led him to do*, she admonished herself.

"Hello, sweetheart," he said.

"You sure look dashing in your new uniform," she said, putting a bright smile on her face as Britt dismounted.

He embraced her tenderly, planted a soft kiss on her lips, and said, "You are a very intelligent young lady."

They had a good laugh together. Then Cherokee Rose asked how it had gone at the office of the chief of police.

"It went quite well. The police chief is a full-blooded Cherokee named Yasson. He and the other officers sure are making me feel welcome on the force."

"Well, I am glad for that. They do not know just how fortunate they are to have you."

Britt went on to tell her that the police department had offices and adjacent jails all over the Territory headed up by men who were called captains. Chief Yasson told him he would be working under Captain Chinando in the office nearest to where he lived…some eleven miles due west of where they stood, near large settlements of Georgia and Tennessee Cherokees.

Cherokee Rose smiled and said, "I am glad the office you work out of will be so close to home."

During supper, Britt filled Walugo in on the news he had given Cherokee Rose. After they had eaten, Walugo looked at his daughter and said, "I will clean up the table and wash the dishes. I want you and Britt to take a walk together. You are going to have less time together once Britt goes on duty."

Both of them thanked him, then walked toward the nearby creek, holding hands. The brilliant setting sun was a perfect half-circle on the horizon, and its golden light was reflected beautifully on the surface of the creek. Soon they were in a wooded area beside the stream and sat down together on the bank.

"Darling, you know how much I think of Sylvia Ward," Cherokee Rose said.

"Mm-hmm."

"Well, today I went to her and asked for her help."

"What kind of help?"

"I asked her to teach me how to be the best wife I can possibly be for you."

By the look that came into Britt's eyes, Cherokee Rose could tell that this touched him deeply.

"I believe you will be the best wife in the whole world anyhow, but what did Sylvia tell you?" he said.

She took a slip of paper out of her dress pocket. "I made some notes to help me remember. She took me to Ephesians chapter 5, and this afternoon I memorized the main verses I am going to be telling you about."

Cherokee Rose went over her notes carefully, quoting the verses of Scripture that went with them.

Britt listened intently until his attention was drawn to a black wolf in the woods across the stream. There was a cardinal in a tree just above the wolf.

Following Britt's line of sight, Cherokee Rose saw the wolf and the red bird. The cardinal was chirping as it looked down at the wolf, and the wolf was quietly looking up at the bird.

After a few minutes, Britt said, "I've never seen anything like this. That wolf and that cardinal seem so friendly toward each other. Isn't that something?"

She smiled at him. "Have you ever heard the legend about the wolf and the redbird?"

He frowned. "A wolf and a redbird? Is this an Indian legend?"

"Yes. A *Cherokee* legend."

"No. I've never heard it, but I'd like to."

"I will tell you the story. Of course, it is only a legend. You will understand that when you hear it. It is said that there was once a wolf whose eyes were sealed shut with pine tar by a raccoon when he was asleep. Upon awaking, the wolf was terrified, not being able to see. He cried for help, and a brown bird nearby came and pecked the tar away. The wolf could see again. In appreciation, the wolf showed the bird a stone in the forest that was wet with red paint. The brown bird liked the color, and painted itself with the paint. The bird that white man calls the cardinal is called the redbird by the Cherokees."

"I have heard the Cherokees talk about the redbird," Britt said, "but I didn't realize it was a cardinal. Nor did I realize there was a legend about how it came into existence."

Britt and Cherokee Rose then did as young couples have done down through the ages. They talked about their plans and dreams for the future: their wedding, their home, and their family. As the sunlight was fading, they held hands and prayed together, asking the Lord to bless their marriage and to give them the number of children He wanted them to have. They promised the Lord that they would bring the children up to love and follow Him.

Soon, they were walking back toward the camp, still holding hands.

$four$

n Sunday, everyone at the open-air church meeting had a wonderful time in both the morning and evening services. In the morning service, more Cherokees—adults and young people—responded to Pastor Ward's preaching, walked forward at invitation time, and were led to Jesus Christ by the counselors. In the evening service, Britt Claiborne was welcomed as a member of the church to the delight of Cherokee Rose, her father, grandparents, and Aunt Tarbee.

Later that night, Walugo said, "Do you recall that I told you a couple of days ago that on Monday I would have to be up and gone before dawn?"

"I will get up extra early and cook your breakfast," Cherokee Rose said.

Walugo smiled. "No need, sweet girl. The Cherokee men and soldiers I am meeting with about building the cabins are planning breakfast together. That way, we can eat and talk at the same time."

Walugo looked at Britt. "If I remember correctly, the soldiers told you they would have your cabin ready by April 20. Is that right?"

"Yes. They know I'm planning to do my share of the construction work by firelight at night, since I'll be on duty six days each week. I'm sure our combined effort will get the cabin ready by April 20."

Walugo smiled. "Well, I have to get my bedroll laid out on the ground."

"Me too," Britt said, and both men walked away.

The fire Cherokee Rose had used to cook supper was still glowing beside the wagon. She went to the fire, sat on the ground, and stared into the dying embers.

Only minutes had passed when Britt came and sat beside her. She smiled at him and said, "I am so eager for us to be in our cabin as husband and wife. Just think—a home of our own."

"Yes. A home of our own."

"It seems like we have traveled a million miles since my parents and I left our home so far away. After all this time in that covered wagon, a home with a solid roof, windows, and a real door will be a dream come true."

Britt took both of her hands in his. "It really will be nice to have a house that doesn't shake and roll with every little gust of wind, won't it?"

"And one that doesn't rock when you move around in it."

Britt chuckled. "Wagons do that, for sure. But you are aware that our cabin won't be as large as the one you and your parents lived in back in North Carolina, aren't you?"

"Yes, I am. But I will make it warm and cozy—a place that you will love coming home to."

"I'm sure you will."

A twinkle flashed in her eyes. "However, sometime in the not too distant future, we may have to consider adding on to it."

"When the Lord gives us children, we will most certainly make room for them."

Cherokee Rose smiled at him. "Well, darling, it is past our bedtime."

Britt rose to his feet, gave her his hand, and helped her stand up.

"I will say good night now," she said. "I am going to go dream about our new cabin. I already have some ideas for how to make it a place of joy and comfort. See you in the morning."

Britt gave her a hug, kissed her tenderly, and said, "Goodnight, sweetheart. I love you."

"I love you, too. Only I love you the most."

He playfully tweaked her nose. "Oh, no, *I* love *you* the most!"

"Impossible," she said as she walked to the wagon and climbed in. True to form, the wagon rocked in response to her weight. She stuck her head through the canvas opening and said, "I hope I can learn to sleep in something that doesn't rock when I enter it."

"You'll do just fine, I'm sure. Now, off to dreamland for you."

Just after breakfast on Monday morning, dressed in his police uniform, Britt was about to mount up and ride to Tahlequah for his first day's schooling so he would be ready to go on duty by Wednesday. As he was hugging Cherokee Rose, they both saw a group of Cherokee men on foot coming toward them, with a dozen soldiers beside them on horseback. Walugo was with them, riding his horse beside the lieutenant who led the soldiers.

When the soldiers and the Indians drew up, Walugo dismounted, stepped up to the couple, and said, "Britt, I have some good news for you."

Britt grinned and raised his eyebrows. "Okay. I can always use some good news."

"These men and I talked about it, and we agreed that since you are now a Territory police officer, you should not have to work at night to help build your cabin. We are going to do *all* the work on it."

"Oh, that *is* good news, Father!" Cherokee Rose said. She smiled at the group. "Thank you!"

The lieutenant set kind eyes on the Indian maiden. "And in spite of the fact that your future husband won't be working on it at night, we will most certainly have the cabin finished by April 20, as promised."

Cherokee Rose's face beamed. "That is wonderful, Lieutenant! That will give me time to make the curtains I have planned and hang them on the windows, as well as having everything else in place before the wedding. I have a chest full of lovely things that were my mother's, which we brought with us from North Carolina."

She looked at Britt. "Oh, it will be such a joy to see Mother's things and to use them! It…well, it will be almost like having her with me again."

Britt patted her cheek, then looked at the group and thanked them for their kindness.

"Oh, Father, thank you!" Cherokee Rose said, taking hold of her father's hand.

Walugo blinked. "For what?"

"Do not play innocent with me. You instigated this offer so Britt would not have to work nights. I just know it!"

Walugo's dark features blushed. "Well…I sort of brought it up to them at breakfast this morning."

Cherokee Rose threw her arms around her father and said, "You are *sneaky*! But I love you for it!"

Britt laughed and cuffed Walugo's chin. "You are sneaky, all right, but I appreciate your thoughtfulness. Working late into the nights on the cabin would make it hard to be at my best when I'm on duty."

When Britt Claiborne arrived home on Tuesday after his second and final day of training, he drew rein at Walugo's wagon and took in the inviting aroma of cooking food and brewing coffee. Cherokee Rose looked up at him while bending over the fire and flipping crisp bacon and fried potatoes in a skillet and gave him a bright smile. "Hello, darling."

While Britt was dismounting, Cherokee Rose set the skillet over the fire and hurried to him. "Hello, yourself," he said picking her up and twirling her around in a circle. After a few seconds of that, he placed her feet on the ground, took her face in his hands, and kissed her soundly.

When he eased back, looking into her eyes, she said, "Britt Claiborne, what is this jubilance all about?"

"Oh, I'm just the happiest man in the world because you are mine!"

They kissed again and then saw Walugo walking toward them from among the other wagons.

"Well, Britt, are you all set to go to work tomorrow?" Walugo asked.

"I'm to report for duty at eight o'clock in the morning."

"Well, gentlemen," Cherokee Rose said, "get your hands washed, and I will have supper ready in a few minutes."

When supper was over, the three of them sat around the fire sipping coffee. The subject returned to the long months on the trail from North Carolina.

"I thought my heart would break the day we packed our few belongings and left the only home I had ever known." Cherokee Rose sighed and set her eyes on Britt. "Little did I know what God had planned for me. Sometimes He takes us through deep, dark valleys to test our faith. Then there is always that glorious mountaintop when we have passed the test, all of it in His perfect time. Never in a million years would I have ever dreamed what His perfect will was for me."

Walugo looked at his daughter. "That is where trusting the Lord, no matter what happens, comes in. It was certainly a long and oftentimes bitter journey, but all the time, the Lord was there in our future. Our heavenly Father had it all planned, just waiting to bring the two of you together."

Britt nodded. "That's right. He was also waiting for *you* to come into my life."

Walugo felt a lump rise in his throat. He managed a smile. "Yes, and you into mine."

Tears welled up in Cherokee Rose's eyes. "Father, I know how much you miss Mother. I…I just do not understand why she was taken from us. I am not angry at the Lord, but I just do not understand."

"Little one, I do not understand either, but the Lord never does wrong. It was all in His plan to take your mother home to heaven when He did. My life here on earth will never be the same without her, but the Lord had His perfect purpose for taking her and leaving me here. Many times in this life, our faith and trust in our heavenly Father weakens, but He has promised that He will never leave us nor forsake us. So, by His grace, we will go on and walk in His will and His way."

"Yes, Father," she said, tears flowing down her cheeks.

Rising to her knees, she wrapped her arms around her father's neck. Walugo was also weeping by then, and their tears mingled as her cheek touched his. Walugo held her close while Britt looked on, struggling with his own tears.

Soon Walugo eased back from his daughter and looked into her eyes. "I know that your mother is smiling down on you from heaven. The fondest wishes she had for you are all about to come true. She wanted so much to see you happily married to the man God chose for you, having your own home, and raising a family. She is at peace, and though you miss her, I want you to be at peace, too, my daughter. Your mother and her sweet ways will always be part of you. Watching you now is so much like having my Naya still with me. You remind me of her so much."

Cherokee Rose patted her father's hand as he continued to hold her gaze. He said in a tender tone, "As God's Word says, 'Weeping may endure for a night, but joy cometh in the morning.' You have had, as it were, your night of weeping, sweet daughter. Now open your heart and let the joy your Lord wants to give you fill your life."

She kissed his cheek. "Oh, I will, Father. And…it pleases me so much to know that I remind you of Mother."

Walugo smiled. "More than I can tell you."

Britt rose to his feet, then knelt down and enveloped both of them in his arms. A tender smile lit up his face as he said, "On that sad day when we left your home in North Carolina, not one of us could have dreamed what the Lord had planned for us. He is such a wonderful heavenly Father. How precious it is to be in His loving care."

Walugo and Cherokee Rose spoke their agreement with Britt's words, then all three stood up, clinging to each other.

"Britt, I am so glad that you will be starting your career as a police officer tomorrow," Cherokee Rose said. "I can tell that you are excited about it."

"That I am. And you know what I'm going to do? I'm going to carry one of my English Bibles and a Cherokee Bible in my saddlebags, so if I ever have opportunity to witness for the Lord, I'll be prepared."

Walugo smiled. "I am so proud of you, Britt. I very much appreciate your desire to bring souls to Jesus."

"And just think," Cherokee Rose said. "Very soon you will be my husband. Oh, the Lord has blessed me so!"

On Wednesday morning, just before eight o'clock, Officer Britt Claiborne rode up to the police office and dismounted. Two full-blooded Indians in uniform came out the door of the office and introduced themselves, saying he had to be the new officer, Britt Claiborne. Britt told them he was, and the two officers wished him the best in his new job, then mounted up and rode away.

When Britt entered the office, he found two men in uniform. One of the men smiled at him and said, "Welcome, Officer Claiborne. I am Captain Chinando. I want you to meet Officer Dan Atkins. He is a quarter Cherokee, just like your papers from Chief Yasson said you are."

After Britt and Dan shook hands, Captain Chinando said,

"Officer Claiborne, I am assigning you to join Officer Atkins in patrolling the area of the Territory that he has ridden since he came on the force. His previous partner's health has been failing, so he resigned from the force last week."

Britt smiled at Dan. "I will be glad to serve as your partner."

"I've read about you in Chief Yasson's report," Dan said, "and I'm glad for the military experience you bring to the job."

"Well, I hope my experience will be an asset."

The new partners then went outside, mounted their horses, and rode toward their assigned portion of the Territory. They were some three miles from the office when they saw a Cherokee man riding hard in their direction. As he drew closer, he spotted their uniforms and signaled for them to stop.

"Blandino, what is wrong?" Dan said, recognizing the man.

"Three white men came on my land less than an hour ago, took several of my steers, and herded them south," Blandino said. "I was on my way to the police station to tell Captain Chinando about it and to ask for help."

"This is my new partner, Officer Britt Claiborne. He and I will go after those rustlers right now."

"Good! I will lead you in the direction the rustlers were taking my cattle."

The three men rode hard, and with Blandino in the lead, they soon caught sight of the three riders herding the steers southward across the plains.

Dan called to Blandino, "Haul up!"

Blandino drew rein and stopped. When the officers came up beside him, Dan said, "Officer Claiborne and I will handle the rustlers. You wait here."

When the three cattle rustlers saw the two uniformed officers riding hard toward them, they drew their revolvers, dismounted, and took cover behind some large rocks.

The bawling cattle made a circle and headed back toward home.

Dan and Britt quickly guided their horses into a dense stand of trees and dismounted. The rustlers started firing at the two lawmen, but the slugs fell short.

"I guess all they have are revolvers." Britt pointed to some other large rocks several yards closer to the cattle thieves. "I've got an idea. Let's go down there, and I'll put my hat on a rock so it looks like I'm right there with you. While you're firing both your revolver and mine, I'll sneak among that heavy brush over there on the right, then come up behind them with my rifle."

Dan nodded. "Great idea! That'll end this standoff in a hurry."

Both officers made a dash for the rocks, firing their revolvers at the rustlers in return. When they reached the rocks, they ducked down behind them, and while Dan was firing at them with his revolver, Britt removed his hat and placed it on a rock. He handed Dan his revolver, then removed his gun belt and holster to give his partner plenty of ammunition. He told him to keep firing, then ducked low in a shallow gully, rifle in hand, and made a run for the brush.

Gunfire filled the air as the three rustlers and Dan Atkins exchanged shots. While Dan kept them occupied, Britt drew up behind them, holding his rifle ready.

When there was a slight lull in the firing, Britt shouted, "Drop your guns!"

All three rustlers spun around, and their faces blanched at what they saw. The black muzzle of the law officer's deadly bolt-action rifle was ready to spit fire. Their eyes darted from side to side like those of trapped animals.

"I said drop those guns!"

Exchanging glances, the trio dropped their guns.

"Hands above your heads!" Britt said.

By that time, Dan Atkins was there, holding both revolvers on the rustlers.

The three men were shackled, placed on their horses, and taken toward the police station. On the way, Dan and Britt learned that they were from Texas, and hoping things would go easier for them if they confessed, they admitted that they had come to Indian Territory to steal cattle.

The rustlers were turned over to Captain Chinando, who locked them up.

Dan and Britt then rode to Blandino's farm and found that he had all of his stolen steers back with his other cattle. He was happy to learn that the rustlers were behind bars.

Captain Chinando, who had the authority to do so, gave the rustlers a long prison sentence for their crime. He sent a messenger to Police Chief Yasson, and early that afternoon, a small unit of soldiers from Fort Gibson came and took the rustlers to the Territory prison, located near Tahlequah.

Late that afternoon, Dan and Britt came upon two groups of young Indians who were in a brawl. One group was made up of Seminoles and the other of Georgia Cherokees. The two police officers had to use force to stop the fighting.

The Cherokees told Dan and Britt that the Seminoles started the fight, threatening the Cherokees and saying they were going to beat them up. The Cherokees said that they tried to keep things peaceful, but the Seminoles forced them to fight.

The Seminoles angrily denied the charges, saying the Cherokees started it. While this was happening, two older Seminole men stepped out from behind some trees and told the officers that the

Cherokees were telling the truth. They both witnessed the whole thing.

The two older Seminoles told Dan and Britt that this bunch of young men from their tribe were known to be troublemakers. They needed to be arrested and punished.

That evening when Britt Claiborne arrived home, Cherokee Rose left the supper she was cooking beside her father's covered wagon and ran to him, opening her arms. After they had embraced, Britt told her about his exciting first day on the job.

When he was giving her the details, fear clutched her heart as she realized the danger he had been in. She pictured the blazing guns of the rustlers and the anger the young Seminole troublemakers must had felt toward her husband and his partner.

A gasp nearly escaped from her lips, but she quickly stifled it with her hand. *I must not show my fear*, she thought. *He does not need to be concerned about me and my feelings when he is on the job, facing whatever peril may come his way.*

At that moment, it was as if the Lord spoke to her in His still, small voice: "*Fear thou not; for I am with thee: be not dismayed; for I am thy God.*"

The fear left Cherokee Rose's heart, and a peaceful smile lit up her face. She reached up, wrapped her arms around Britt's neck, and kissed his cheek. "Welcome home, my love. Welcome home. I am so glad you are all right. I have prayed for you many times during the day, and I will do so every day you are on duty."

Britt held her tight. "Thank you, sweetheart. That means more to me than I could ever tell you."

five

t breakfast on Thursday morning, while a chilly breeze swept
across the rolling prairie, Britt
Claiborne told Cherokee Rose and her father
all about his assigned partner, Officer Dan
Atkins. He told them that Dan was a quarter
Cherokee, was in his early sixties and a wid-
ower, and that he had been a town marshal
in three different Kansas towns. He also said
Dan was a likable man and that, for his age,
he carried himself quite well as a lawman.

"I am glad you have a partner that you
like," Walugo said.

"I want both of you to pray that I'll be able to talk with Dan about the gospel and that eventually I'll be able to lead him to the Lord."

Both Walugo and his daughter told Britt they would pray for Dan's salvation.

When breakfast was over, Britt saddled Blackie, tied a canteen of fresh water onto the saddle, and led him to where Cherokee Rose, wearing a light buckskin jacket, stood near the wagon. She held a large blue and white cloth napkin wrapped around the lunch she had prepared for him.

Britt smiled when he saw the napkin. "So what am I having for lunch today?"

She handed the folded napkin to him. "Well, there are four large, thick slices of bread, some cold roast beef, and a slab of cheese."

A broad grin spread over Britt's face. He shook the napkin slightly, as if testing its weight. "My, my. There must be enough food in here for three or four men."

"Well-l-l, I can't have my man going hungry. You could share some of it with your partner if it is too much for you."

Britt bent down and placed a soft kiss on her cheek. "If Dan looks like he's starving, I might do that. Now, you need to hurry and get inside the wagon. It's still right nippy out here this morning. I'll see you around suppertime."

Britt placed his lunch in a saddlebag, hugged Cherokee Rose, and said, "I love you."

"I love you, too," she said. "And I will be asking the Lord to give you a good opportunity to witness to Dan. And praying for your safety."

Britt thanked her, then climbed in the saddle and put Blackie in motion. When he was about forty yards from her, he looked back at Cherokee Rose and waved. She threw him a kiss and waved in return.

He then put his faithful steed to a fast trot. Cherokee Rose wrapped her arms around herself, shivering in the cold breeze. She watched Britt until he rounded a bend near a stand of trees.

With a smile gracing her pretty face, she hummed a nameless tune and climbed back into the wagon to do some much-needed mending on one of her buckskin skirts.

The hours passed in relative quiet as Britt Claiborne and Dan Atkins rode their patrol that morning. Periodically, they met up with Indians who were on horseback or driving their wagons and stopped to chat with them. Cattle herds were numerous in the pastures where the grass was beginning to turn green. On several occasions, they came upon Tennessee and Georgia Cherokees plowing their fields, getting ready to plant their crops. They paused to greet them, then rode on.

At noon, they stopped to eat. When Dan saw the lunch that Cherokee Rose had prepared for Britt, he chuckled and said that she must have meant some of that food for his partner.

Britt looked at the meager lunch Dan had prepared for himself and said, "I'm sure she did, pal. I'll be glad to share it with you."

When they mounted up to ride on, both men were comfortably full.

Soon they were circling back toward the area where the North Carolina Cherokees had settled. It was midafternoon when they caught sight of a wagon off to their right racing across the prairie, being pulled by two galloping horses. The wagon was bouncing and fishtailing dangerously. Dan and Britt could see a Cherokee man at the reins with a woman beside him. She was gripping the seat, trying to keep from being tossed from the bounding wagon.

Dan looked at Britt, eyes wide. "We'd better see if we can help that man get those horses stopped."

Britt nodded, and they put their mounts to a gallop.

Suddenly they saw the right front wheel of the wagon drop into a hole in the ground, and both the man and the woman were thrown from the wagon seat. The harnesses tore loose, and the team galloped away, dragging harness fragments behind them.

As Dan and Britt drew near the spot where the man and woman lay on the ground, Britt immediately recognized them.

Durabo and Nannalee were in their late fifties. They had been on the journey from North Carolina to Indian Territory, and Britt had gotten to know them well. He knew Nannalee especially well because she attended all the preaching services on the journey, and was now a member of the church Layne Ward pastored. Durabo was not a Christian and never attended any of the preaching services on the journey.

When the police officers pulled rein, Nannalee was rising to her knees and looking at her husband, who lay on his back several feet from her. He was not moving.

Shaking violently and gasping for breath, Nannalee tried to stand up, but fell back on the hard ground with a moan. By this time, Britt was off his horse and kneeling over her. Her face was pale and wore an expression of horror. Suddenly she focused on Britt and said, "Oh, Britt! Please help me! Durabo is hurt bad!"

"You know these people?" Dan said.

Britt nodded. "They were on the journey from North Carolina with me." He took hold of Nannalee's hand. "Are you all right?"

Her pallid face wore an expression of fear. "I…do not think I am seriously hurt, but Durabo looks bad."

Britt helped Nannalee to her feet and guided her to where her husband lay on the ground. Durabo, his face ashen, looked up at them and seemed to recognize Britt.

Nannalee fell to her knees beside Durabo and laid her hand on his forehead, where a large gash was bleeding profusely. At the same time, she saw blood on his pant leg and that his leg was at an odd angle.

Britt knelt beside her and said, "Durabo, can you move your head? Your arms and legs?"

Durabo worked his mouth painfully. "No. I…I cannot move at all."

Nannalee pulled a large bandanna from her dress pocket and pressed it against the gash in his forehead. Holding it there, she pulled his pant leg up with her free hand and gasped. Splintered bone was sticking through the flesh.

"We'll need to make a tourniquet for his leg," Britt said. "I'll rip off part of his other pant leg and use it for that."

Britt quickly tore off a length of the pant leg and began to wrap it around Durabo's injured leg.

Dan Atkins knelt down, looked at Nannalee, and asked, "What caused your horses to go into that wild gallop, ma'am?"

"While we were traveling across the prairie, we suddenly came upon a large nest of rattlesnakes. The horses shied and then bolted."

Britt cinched the tourniquet tightly and looked down into Durabo's glazed eyes. "The bleeding will stop soon. I've done lots of tourniquets on battlefields. Now…I want you to try to raise your head just a little."

Durabo gritted his teeth and made the attempt, but his head did not move. "I cannot."

"Can you move your hands?"

Durabo was still for a moment, then said, "I have no feeling below my neck. Nothing will move."

Britt looked at Nannalee. "I'm afraid his neck may be broken."

Nannalee's face lost what color it had. "Oh, no. He…he could die right here!"

Durabo'e eyes widened and went to Nannalee. He looked at her steadily as she said to Britt, "My husband is not a Christian. I have talked to him many times about Jesus dying for sinners, but he has shown no interest."

"I'll be right back," Britt said.

Nannalee and Dan watched Britt as he ran to his horse.

Blackie whinnied as Britt opened one of the saddlebags and took out both the Cherokee Bible and the English Bible. He hurried back to Durabo, knelt beside him, and asked how well he knew English. Nannalee answered for him. "We both know English quite well."

Britt handed the Cherokee Bible to Nannalee and said, "Hold this for me, then, will you? Durabo, I want to read to you what God says about eternity…about heaven and hell."

Britt read passage after passage on heaven and hell, then read about man's guilt before God and how His Son died on the cross to provide the way of salvation for a world of lost sinners.

Dan listened intently and grew quite tense.

"Britt, excuse me for butting in," Dan said, "but we're going to have to take this man where he can get medical aid. The doctor at Fort Gibson has treated many sick and injured Indians. I know he'll help Durabo. I'll go to the nearest farm and see if I can borrow a team and wagon so we can transport him to the fort."

Britt sensed Dan's nervousness, and looked up and said, "Thanks, my friend. Please hurry."

As Dan mounted his horse and rode away, Britt continued to

talk about the plan of salvation. Durabo, who obviously feared that he was dying, listened intently, and when Britt asked if he understood his need to be saved, Durabo blinked at the tears that filled his eyes and said, "Yes, I do, Britt. I have been so wrong not to listen to Nannalee when she has tried to get me to see my need to know the Lord Jesus Christ as my Saviour. I want to be saved."

Nannalee looked on with tears streaming down her cheeks as Durabo called on the Lord to save him. Hardly had he done so, when his eyes closed, and he breathed out his last breath.

Tears flowed as Nannalee sat down on the ground, raised her husband's head onto her lap, and cradled him in her arms.

Britt put an arm around her shoulder and did all he could to comfort her. He quoted several Scriptures for her to cling to, and though she was deeply disturbed, a fresh, new peace filled her aching heart. She knew Durabo was now with Jesus in heaven.

Nannalee looked up at Britt, wiped tears, and said, "I am so glad you did not hesitate to talk to him before it was too late. I do not know what I would have done if he had died lost and gone to hell. Now, knowing that I will see him again in heaven, I can go on with my life and have contentment in my heart." Nannalee held her husband's head close to her heart, placed a tender kiss on his lips, and said in a soft whisper, "I will see you in heaven, my dear one. I love you."

At that moment, they heard pounding hooves and the sound of a rattling vehicle. They looked up to see Dan Atkins pulling up in a wagon he had borrowed from nearby Cherokee farmers.

Britt stepped up to him as he reined in and said, "We won't need to go to the fort, Dan. Durabo just died."

Dan's lips pulled into a thin line. "I'm sorry." His eyes went to Nannalee, who was sitting on the ground, holding her husband. "How's she taking it?"

"Quite well, actually. She knows that because Durabo received the Lord Jesus Christ as his Saviour, he is now in heaven."

Dan bit his lips as he left the wagon seat. He walked to where Nannalee sat on the ground and said, "You have my condolences, ma'am. I'm sorry your husband died."

She looked up at him and forced a faint smile. "Thank you."

The next morning, Dan and Britt took time off from their patrolling to attend Durabo's funeral service, which Pastor Layne Ward conducted at the local burial ground.

A great number of North Carolina Cherokees were there, and as Pastor Ward began his message at the graveside, he said, "All of you who are Christians will be glad to know that yesterday, before Durabo died, Officer Britt Claiborne had the joy of leading him to the Lord. It's a tremendous blessing for Nannalee to know that her husband is now in heaven."

There were many amens as the Christians in the crowd expressed their joy at the good news. This brought a smile from Nannalee, who was standing with Sylvia Ward near the open grave.

After Durabo had been buried and Pastor Ward finished the service, the Cherokee people filed by Nannalee to offer their condolences. Those who were Christians expressed their delight that one day Nannalee would be rejoined with her husband in heaven.

When Cherokee Rose stepped up to Nannalee with Britt and Walugo at her side, she embraced her tenderly, then looked into her tear-dimmed eyes and said, "Nannalee, we would love to have you come and eat lunch with us. That is, if you feel up to it."

Nannalee caressed Cherokee Rose's cheek and said, "Thank you for the offer, but there is much to do at my place, and with my wagon broken, I will need to somehow have it repaired quickly so

I have a place to live until my cabin is built."

"You are more than welcome to stay with us until you can get your wagon repaired. I am the only one who sleeps in Father's wagon, so there is room."

"Nannalee, I will try to arrange my schedule so I can repair your wagon for you," Britt said.

"No need, Britt," Walugo said. "Your schedule is a heavy one. I will get some of my farmer friends to help me, and we will have that wagon repaired in a few days."

Nannalee smiled at him. "Oh, thank you, Walugo. And Britt, once more I want to thank you for leading my husband to Jesus."

Britt patted her shoulder. "I'm just so glad the Lord let me be there so I could do it. And since my future father-in-law is going to see that your wagon gets fixed, if there's ever anything else I can do for you, please let me know."

She nodded. "I will do that. Thank you."

Nannalee then turned to Cherokee Rose, hugged her, and said, "I have some Christian neighbors who live close to my wagon. Let me see what arrangements I can make for the few days until it is repaired. If I need a place to stay, I will come to you. And, sweet girl…thank you for caring."

Cherokee Rose kissed her cheek. "I love you. That is why I care."

Others were in line to speak to the new widow. As Cherokee Rose, Britt, and Walugo walked away, Britt said, "I want you two to keep praying for my partner. He heard some of what I said to Durabo, and since then, he has tried to avoid any talk about the Bible, the Lord, or eternity."

Both Cherokee Rose and her father assured Britt that they would be praying for Dan.

ↄ

When the mourners had all left the grave site, Pastor Ward and his wife told Nannalee that they would walk her back to her wagon. She thanked them for the offer, but told them she wanted to stay at the grave alone for a while. Sylvia hugged her and said she understood.

Nannalee stood alone over the grave and prayed, thanking the Lord for bringing Durabo to salvation and asking for strength to go on in life without her husband.

She then squared her shoulders, turned, and headed toward the circles of wagons and tents. She pulled her shawl up tightly around her neck as the cool wind once again swept over the lonesome prairie.

When Dan Atkins and Britt Claiborne were once again on patrol, Britt guided the conversation to Durabo's having become a Christian just before he died.

"I don't mean to offend you, Britt," Dan said, "but I'm having a hard time believing that a man can just up and get religion a few minutes before he dies, then go to heaven. I figure any man or woman would have to do some good works after getting religion in order to deserve to go to heaven."

"Can we stop for a little while so I can show you the truth about this from the Scriptures?" Britt said.

"Yeah. I guess we can stop for a few minutes, anyway."

They guided their horses into a wooded area and dismounted. Britt took the English Bible out of his saddlebag, and they sat down on a fallen tree.

Using the Bible, Britt showed Dan that salvation was by grace, not by good works. He made it clear that no one could ever deserve to go to heaven. Everyone needed salvation, not religion.

"Well, I don't see how a man can just believe, then die and go to heaven," Dan said.

Britt turned to the Gospel of Luke and showed Dan the account of the two thieves who were crucified at the same time Jesus was. He pointed out how the repentant thief turned to Jesus and asked Him to save him…and how Jesus promised him right then and there that the two of them would be together in paradise that very day.

"See, Dan, that thief *did* believe on Jesus for salvation a few minutes before he died, and Jesus saved him."

Dan was silent for a moment, then said, "Britt, I don't mean to offend you, but I'm just not interested in this salvation stuff."

Britt looked him square in the eye. "You *will* be when it is too late, Dan. Let me show you another Scripture that'll help—"

"We need to get back on patrol," Dan cut in, standing to his feet.

Britt stood up and closed his Bible. "All right, my friend. I guess we'd better be going."

six

s the weeks passed and the Claiborne cabin was being built by their Cherokee friends and the soldiers from Fort Gibson, Officers Britt Claiborne and Dan Atkins were kept busy arresting Indians who broke the law and white men who infringed on Indian land and property.

Cherokee Rose spent her days cooking, cleaning her father's wagon, and doing the wash in the clear, cool stream nearby, all the time dreaming about the day when she would finally become Mrs. Britt Claiborne. There was always a prayer in her heart for Britt's safety, and at the end of each day, she rejoiced and thanked the Lord when she saw him come riding in, safe and sound once again.

On the next weekday Britt had off, he and Cherokee Rose planned to borrow Walugo's wagon and team and drive to the large general store in Tahlequah, where they could purchase material for curtains, as well as bedding, a stove, and other items for their new home.

They had hired two Cherokee men to make their furniture and had a good time picturing what the cabin would look like when they were married and living there.

One day in the second week of April, while Dan and Britt were on patrol together, Britt felt the urge to talk to Dan once more about his need to receive Jesus as his Saviour. Dan was polite, but told Britt he was not interested in becoming a Christian.

Britt quoted Scripture after Scripture on the horror of a person facing God in judgment for having rejected His Son and spending eternity in the lake of fire. Still, Dan showed no fear and told Britt that he could die as valiantly as any Christian could. Death did not frighten him.

That evening Britt shared Dan's words with Cherokee Rose and Walugo, and they said they would pray that the Lord would use the Scriptures Britt had given him to break down Dan's defenses and draw him to Jesus.

On Tuesday, April 16, Britt borrowed Walugo's wagon and team and took Cherokee Rose to the general store in Tahlequah. While he was in one part of the store looking at woodstoves, Cherokee Rose was in the fabric section, examining bolt after bolt of curtain material, trying to decide which she liked best for the cabin windows.

She finally decided on the material she liked best and carried a bolt to the counter to be measured and cut. She also purchased some new needles, thread, and some trim material, as well as a small multicolored rag rug for the bedroom.

When that purchase was completed, Cherokee Rose placed the items in the spacious basket-on-wheels she had found at the front door. She still had bedding to buy, as well as towels, washcloths, lye soap, a mop and bucket, a broom, dust cloths, cups, saucers, dishes, skillets and pans, eating utensils, and other kitchen supplies.

She had just finished her purchasing and was wheeling the heavily loaded basket toward the counter at the front of the store when Britt came up beside her, pulling a large cart. On it were a cookstove for the kitchen, a woodstove for heating the cabin, plus lanterns and kerosene.

Cherokee Rose smiled at him. "Oh, Officer Claiborne," she said in a teasing tone, "I was just wondering how I was ever going to get all these items out to the wagon. I am so glad you came along!"

Britt laughed and ran his gaze over her overloaded basket. "Wow! Did you buy out the store?"

"Oh, I left a little on each shelf, but who knows? I may be back for that later!"

By midafternoon on Saturday, April 20, the Claiborne cabin was finished. The two Georgia Cherokee men placed the furniture they had made inside the cabin. With the help of one of his North Carolina Cherokee friends, Walugo put the stoves in place, and Cherokee Rose hung the curtains on the windows.

Late that afternoon when Britt came riding up to the wagon after a long day on patrol, Cherokee Rose was standing there, her face beaming. "Hello, love of my life," she said with a lilt in her voice. "The cabin is all done and ready for your inspection. Want to go and see it?"

Britt dismounted and said, "I sure do!"

Cherokee Rose did a hop and a skip in the direction of their cabin. Looking back over her shoulder, she giggled and said, "Come on, slowpoke!"

Britt picked up his pace and took her by the hand. She still stayed a half step ahead of him, making him reach forward to keep hold of her hand. When they reached the cabin, she pulled her hand from his, dashed onto the porch, and opened the door.

When Britt entered the cabin, he stopped and looked around as Cherokee Rose drew up to his side.

"Oh, sweetheart!" he said. "It's beautiful!"

The small parlor had a warm fire in the woodstove, casting a soft glow over the room. Two kerosene lanterns were burning on small tables that sided two brown horsehair chairs facing the woodstove.

On one wall was a small curio unit of shelves, which the Georgia Cherokee men had built at Cherokee Rose's request. She had placed some of her mother's precious keepsakes on them.

The window curtains were a tan and light blue design and now were tied back with dark brown tassels.

Britt sighed. "This is fantastic, sweetheart. I know we're going to spend many happy, comfortable hours in this room."

"I am glad you like it," she said, her face beaming. "Welcome home, Officer Claiborne!" She then took him by the hand. "Let me guide you further on the tour."

Stepping to a closed door a few feet away, Cherokee Rose

opened it and led him into the bedroom. The four-poster bed took up most of the room, but she had managed to fit in a washstand—also built by the Georgia Cherokees—with a blue and white pitcher and bowl sitting on a white crocheted doily, which she had secretly made. A small clothes cabinet stood in one corner, and a white painted rocking chair sat in front of the window. A blue and white coverlet adorned the bed, and on the floor beside the bed was the multicolored rag rug she had purchased at the general store.

"It's beautiful," Britt said. "This place shines with your loving care."

She looked up at him with a glint in her eye and pointed to a small open space in one corner. "When the Lord gives us our first baby, a crib can go right there. But shortly thereafter, we will have to add on a room or two for our children."

Britt smiled at her as she took his hand in hers and led him into the kitchen.

"This room is *really* my pride and joy." Cherokee Rose let go of his hand and twirled around the kitchen, stopping by the cookstove. "Oh, Britt, I am so glad to have a stove! I will no longer have to cook over an open fire on the ground. It is like a dream come true!"

"Praise the Lord!" he said, his own face beaming.

In the center of the kitchen was a good-sized table with four brightly painted blue chairs around it. Part of one wall housed a tall cupboard painted the same bright blue as the chairs.

On the opposite wall, next to the shiny black cookstove, was a wide shelf for preparing meals and baking. Snow-white starched curtains adorned the outdoor scene framed by a window on the west side of the room. Cherokee Rose walked toward the window, and Britt followed her.

"Darling," she said, "now I can take in the colorful sunsets as they settle over the rolling hills. And on rainy or snowy days, I can watch the storms blow in from the west." She wrapped her arms around him. "Oh, Britt, thank you for our cozy home! We will be so happy and content here."

She raised up on tiptoe and planted a soft kiss on his lips.

He held her close and said, "We most certainly will be happy and content in our home, sweetheart. The Lord be praised!"

"Yes, the Lord be praised!"

To Cherokee Rose, the days seemed to drag by, even though there was much to do. Saturday, April 27, seemed especially slow in passing, but when she awakened on Sunday morning just before dawn, she sat up in her bed inside the wagon and said, "Oh, thank You, Lord, it is finally here! Today I will become Britt's wife!"

Some time before the first rays of the sun cast their brilliance across the rolling prairie, Cherokee Rose slipped out of the wagon and hurried to the nearby creek and the secluded spot set aside for the women and girls.

The water was chilly, but soon she had bathed, washed her long, luxurious hair, put her clothing back on, and hurried back to the wagon before anyone else in the camp was stirring. Inside the wagon, she used a thick towel to dry her hair, then brushed out the tangles and let it completely dry.

Cherokee Rose prepared a hasty breakfast while Britt and her father lit the cook-fire, and soon thereafter they were gathered for the regular Sunday morning Sunday school and preaching service. When the morning service was over, Pastor Layne Ward reminded the congregation that the Britt Claiborne–Cherokee Rose wedding would take place at three o'clock that afternoon.

Chief Bando and Nevarra had invited Britt, Cherokee Rose,

and Walugo to eat Sunday dinner with them. Both Britt and Cherokee Rose ate very little, and the others at the table understood why.

As soon as the meal was over, Cherokee Rose kissed the cheeks of her grandparents, her father, and her husband-to-be, then hurried to her father's covered wagon and climbed inside. She drew the canvas flaps closed, then opened a drawer in the crude chest that sat at the rear of the wagon bed and carefully took out her wedding dress.

Some ten days earlier, her grandmother, Nevarra, had surprised her by presenting her with the soft doeskin wedding dress she had made for her. It was bleached white and was complete with beading and fringe.

Tears filmed the bride's eyes as she held the dress close to her heart, remembering how she had shed grateful tears and embraced her grandmother when she had presented it to her. She then held it at arm's length and marveled at its beauty. "Oh, Britt," she whispered as if he were there, "I hope you love it as much as I do."

Cherokee Rose put the dress on and slipped her feet into the soft, knee-high bleached buckskin moccasins her father had given her only three days before. As she was lacing up the moccasins, she heard a familiar female voice at the rear of the wagon.

"Cherokee Rose, are you in there?"

"Yes, Grandmother," she called. "Please come in and tell me if I look all right."

Nevarra parted the canvas flaps and climbed inside. A tiny gasp escaped her mouth as she beheld her granddaughter standing before her in the wedding dress and moccasins. The bride's face was beaming, capped off with a brilliant smile.

"Oh, you look so lovely, my child!" Nevarra said. "The happiness is glowing from your face!" She gave her granddaughter a hug, then stepped back. "We had better go. A large crowd awaits this most happy occasion."

Cherokee Rose pulled Nevarra to her, kissed her cheek, and looked into her black eyes. "I love you, Grandmother. Thank you for all that you are to me."

"I love you too, my little one. You are such a sweet blessing in my life."

They looked into each other's eyes for a moment, then Cherokee Rose climbed down from the rear of the wagon. Nevarra followed her, and they walked toward the spot where the crowd was gathering.

As they drew closer, they saw Walugo waiting for them. Nevarra smiled at him, then parted from the bride, allowing her father to walk her the rest of the way.

As father and daughter moved up the aisle that the crowd had formed for them, Cherokee Rose's eyes fell on her groom as he waited at the front between Pastor Layne Ward and Pastor Jesse Bushyhead.

Holding on to her father's arm, Cherokee Rose looked heavenward and moved her lips soundlessly, saying, "It is happening, Mother, just as you said it would. I love you."

With that, she continued on toward the love of her life, the man who in only minutes would be her husband.

It was a warm, cloudless day as Pastor Ward performed the ceremony. He had his close friend Pastor Bushyhead pray for the bride and groom after they had said their vows and had been pronounced husband and wife.

First to approach the newlyweds and congratulate them was Walugo. He kissed his daughter's cheek and said, "Your mother is among the great cloud of witnesses in heaven and has been watching the wedding. I know she is very happy for you."

The bride's eyes filled with tears. "Yes, Father. And one day we will be together with her, never to part again."

Walugo blinked at his own tears, then embraced Britt and said to Cherokee Rose, "I am so glad that the Lord brought Britt into your life. Welcome into our family, *son*."

Britt smiled. "Thank you, *Father*!"

Walugo stepped aside to allow other family members and friends to approach the bride and groom.

Pastor Layne Ward and Sylvia waited to be the last to come to Britt and Cherokee Rose. They spent a few minutes talking together, then Pastor Ward had the four of them join hands, and he led in prayer for the newlyweds as they began their life together.

The ladies of the North Carolina Cherokee community had prepared a feast for all who attended the wedding, and Pastor and Sylvia Ward led the bride and groom to the loaded tables.

The young couple ate and mingled with their many friends, accepting and enjoying more good wishes.

It had been a beautiful spring day, but as evening approached, the air turned a bit chilly, and Britt wrapped his arm around his bride.

"No one will leave until we do, sweetheart," he whispered in her ear. "I think it's time for us to go to our cabin."

She looked up at him, a tender smile lighting her dark brown eyes. "I think you are right, my dear husband."

They waved at their family members and friends, and arms around each other, they headed toward their cabin as the last light of the setting sun glowed on the horizon.

As Britt and his bride walked toward their cabin together, he told her that in the white man's world, the groom always carried the bride across the threshold of their home after the wedding ceremony.

"Since I'm three-quarters white man," he said, smiling down at her, "I'm going to honor this tradition."

"Can the three-quarters of white man in you manage to carry me over the threshold, or will it take all four quarters?"

Britt laughed. "As tiny as you are, I could carry you a hundred miles with just my Cherokee quarter!"

When they drew up to the cabin, Britt said, "All right, Mrs. Claiborne, it's time for your husband to carry you over the threshold of our new house."

Cherokee Rose wrapped her arms around her husband's neck as he swept her into his arms and carried her toward the front door.

arly on Monday morning, April 29, Britt Claiborne was building a fire in the kitchen stove while his new bride stood at the wide shelf next to the stove, getting ready to prepare pancake batter for breakfast.

Cherokee Rose Claiborne smiled at her new groom and said, "I am sure glad Captain Chinando gave you today off as a wedding present. It will be nice to have one whole day with my husband after our wedding."

The fire was crackling in the stove as Britt placed the heavy metal lid on the firebox. "It sure will be nice to have the whole day with you, sweetheart." As he spoke, Britt stepped to his wife, folded her into his arms, and kissed her soundly.

There was a knock at the front door of the cabin. They looked at each other, eyes wide, and Cherokee Rose said, "Who could that be so early in the morning?"

Britt shrugged his wide shoulders and headed toward the front of the cabin. "I don't know, but we will soon find out."

Britt swung the door open, and there stood Chief Bando, a big smile on his lips. "Good morning, Britt," he said, glancing past him to his granddaughter. "And good morning to *you*, Mrs. Claiborne."

Cherokee Rose was now moving toward the door. "Good morning, Grandfather."

Britt was about to invite Bando in when the chief said, "I've been waiting a short distance from the cabin, and as soon as I saw the smoke rising from your kitchen stove, I knew it was all right to knock on your door. Nevarra is preparing breakfast for the four of us, and I am here to ask you to come and eat with us."

"Oh, Grandfather, you and Grandmother are so thoughtful!" Cherokee Rose turned to her husband. "What do you think, Britt? Do you want to eat breakfast with my grandparents?"

"Well, since you haven't started ours as yet, I think it would be a great idea!"

At the Bando cabin, when they were finishing breakfast, Bando said, "You newlyweds can take a seat over there in the parlor area. I will help your grandmother clean up the kitchen and wash the dishes. Then we will walk you back to your cabin."

Cherokee Rose shook her head. "Oh, no, Grandfather, I will help her. And you certainly do not need to walk us back to our cabin. You and Britt sit down in the parlor. As soon as Grandmother and I get the kitchen work done, Britt and I will—"

"Now, sweet girl," Bando said, "it is not right for you to help with the dishes on the day after your wedding. You and Britt sit down. There is no need to hurry away."

Britt smiled. "Pardon me, Chief, but it seems to me that you two are wanting to delay our return to the cabin."

"It does? What would make you think that?"

"Well, it just looks that way." He gave Bando a suspicious look. "You aren't pulling a trick on us are you?"

"Why, of course not. We simply want you to stay here with us a little longer, and then we will walk you to your cabin."

"You have something 'up your sleeve,' as white men say, Grandfather," Cherokee Rose said. "I can tell."

Bando and Nevarra exchanged glances, then Nevarra said, "Cherokee Rose, if you want to help me with the dishes and cleaning up the kitchen, that will be fine. You men go sit in the parlor."

When all the work in the kitchen was done, Bando and Nevarra joined the newlyweds as they headed for the Claiborne cabin.

Both Britt and Cherokee Rose were still playfully needling her grandparents about having some ulterior motive for inviting them to breakfast and delaying their return home when they rounded a corner on the path and came within sight of their cabin. The newlyweds both stopped when they saw several members of their church in front of the cabin, smiling and waiting for them. At the forefront were the pastor and his wife.

Britt looked at Bando and Nevarra. "Now I *know* you two had an ulterior motive for your actions this morning."

Bando shrugged his shoulders. "Well, let us go see what this is all about."

As they drew up to the crowd, Pastor Layne Ward smiled and said, "The people of our church have gone together and bought a wedding present for the bride."

At that moment, two men of the church came around the Claiborne cabin. One of them was leading Britt's horse, Blackie, and the other was leading a magnificent white mare. The man leading the mare drew up to Cherokee Rose and said, "Mrs. Claiborne, Blackie now shares his corral with his bride. Her name is White Star."

Cherokee Rose saw that the mare was wearing a nice bridle and saddle. Putting fingertips to her lips, she looked around at the crowd and said, "Oh, she is beautiful. Thank you so much!"

"Yes, thank you," Britt said. "Now my wife and I can go riding together."

Cherokee Rose stepped up to White Star and hugged her long neck. The mare bobbed her head and whinnied softly.

With a hand on White Star's neck, Cherokee Rose looked at the people again. This time there were tears misting her eyes. "All of you are so gracious. Please accept my deep gratitude."

The Claibornes settled down in their new cabin. Cherokee Rose stayed busy every day, and while doing her housework, she often prayed that the Lord would protect her husband in his police work. At the close of each day, when Britt arrived home, she praised the Lord in her heart that He had kept His hand on Britt through the dangers he faced.

Since the sun was setting later in the day as spring moved slowly toward summer, Britt and Cherokee Rose took rides together after supper each evening. Cherokee Rose dearly loved White Star, and they were growing closer to each other day by day.

One day as they were riding alongside the creek near their home, Cherokee Rose said, "How is it going with Dan Atkins? Have you seen any changes in his attitude toward the Lord and the gospel?"

"Well, from time to time I still bring up his need to open his heart to Jesus, but Dan says he has no fear of death. He argues that he has no need of salvation."

"Well, the Lord has broken through harder cases than Dan Atkins," Cherokee Rose said. "I will just keep praying for him."

"Me too, honey. My God can break through Dan's foolish unbelief and make him listen to the truth."

"He most certainly can," she said. "Race you back to the cabin."

Britt grinned. "All right. Blackie and I always like a challenge."

The next day, after Britt had ridden away to work, Cherokee Rose was humming the melody to "Amazing Grace" while doing the washing in a tub that she had filled with steaming hot water from pans on her kitchen stove.

Her heart was happy, and she smiled to herself as she thought of how she and White Star had won the race against Britt and Blackie the evening before. She felt sure that Britt kept Blackie in check enough to let her win, but he would never admit it.

"Lord," she said, her hands deep in the sudsy water, "You have given me such a wonderful husband. Thank You. I love him so much. This is what I have been wanting ever since I was a little girl."

She picked up one of Britt's shirts from the water and scrubbed it vigorously. "Mother taught me so well, even when I was very young, how to manage a home, how to cook and sew, and now I have my own home. Thank You, Lord, for being so good to me."

Soon she finished her washing and hung it on the thin rope line that Britt had strung for her between two posts. Returning to the kitchen, she kneaded bread dough that she had set to rising earlier. She then divided the dough into four loaves, placed them in pans, and slid them into the oven. Soon, the entire cabin was redolent with the mouth-watering aroma of baking bread.

The days passed quickly, and each evening Cherokee Rose listened for the familiar sound of Britt's horse. When he rode up to the cabin, she was always out the door, ready to greet him with a hug and a kiss when he dismounted. While he was leaving the saddle, she would thank her heavenly Father that her husband was home safe again.

During the next few weeks, the Tennessee, Georgia, and Alabama Cherokees brought milk cows, beef cattle, and corn and wheat seed as gifts to the North Carolina Cherokees. They also took many of the North Carolina Cherokee men hunting, and they did well bringing home meat for their families. The North Carolina Cherokees were becoming happier in their new home in Indian Territory. They enjoyed the companionship of the other Cherokee tribes, as well as that of the Chickasaw, the Choctaw, the Creek, and the Seminole.

One day in late August, the chiefs from the Tennessee, Georgia, and Alabama Cherokees rode into the North Carolina Cherokee area. They were welcomed by many of the people, and Chief Kiwano of the Georgia Cherokees asked if Chief John Ross was at home. Kiwano was told that John Ross was working in the yard around his new cabin and was given directions so they could find him.

Moments later, two teenage boys ran to Ross's cabin and found him cutting weeds near the front porch.

Ross looked up and smiled at the boys. "Hello, Waturi. Hello, Atcando."

"Chief John Ross, there are a whole bunch of Cherokee chiefs here to see you!" Waturi said. "What do you suppose they want?"

"I have no idea, but we will soon find out. Here they come now."

The two boys stepped back a few yards as the chiefs rode up and John Ross welcomed them. He knew all of them well because of his long position of leadership amongst the entire Cherokee Nation.

The chiefs dismounted, and Waturi and Atcando listened as the chiefs told Ross that they were amazed at how well the children were doing in the Cherokee Nation schools, all because they had the Cherokee alphabet Chief Sequoyah had created.

"Chief John Ross," Chief Kiwano said, "all of us agree that the Cherokee Nation is much stronger because of what Chief Sequoyah did in giving us our own written language. We have come to you because we would like to have a special meeting to honor Chief Sequoyah. Do you think the North Carolina chiefs will want to join us?"

"I am positive they will," Ross said.

"We thought they would," Kiwano said. "All of us have already agreed that we want *you* to head up this special meeting."

John Ross smiled from ear to ear. "I would be glad to lead in this effort, my friends. When would you like to have the meeting?"

"We have all agreed that it should be in early September," Chief Vandigo said.

"All right," Ross said. "Once we settle on a date, I will contact all of the North Carolina chiefs about the meeting. I will also tell them it is to be kept secret from Chief Sequoyah so it will be a surprise to him."

On the morning of September 10, Chief Sequoyah was sweeping the floor in his cabin when he glanced out a front window and saw Chief John Ross approaching his front door. He laid the broom aside, opened the door, and said with a smile, "Good morning, Chief John Ross."

"Good morning to you, my friend," Ross said. "I came by to tell you that there is going to be a special meeting today at two o'clock at our regular meeting place."

Sequoyah blinked. "Oh? Who all will attend the meeting, and what is it for?"

"Well, all I can tell you is that it is an important meeting and we need you to be there. I will come to your cabin a few minutes before two so we can walk to the meeting together. When we get there, you will have your questions answered."

Sequoyah shrugged his shoulders. "All right. I guess I will have to go just to find out what this is all about."

That afternoon, when John Ross and Sequoyah were walking toward the meeting place together, Sequoyah was stunned to see so many Cherokees gathering. He looked at Ross. "That is a very large crowd, Chief John Ross."

Ross nodded. "There are Cherokees here from the Tennessee, Georgia, and Alabama clans as well as our North Carolina Cherokees."

When they reached the meeting place, Sequoyah took a seat near the front of the crowd with some of his friends.

At precisely two o'clock, Chief John Ross faced the crowd and spoke loudly to be heard by all. "I am happy to welcome you to this meeting." He glanced at Chief Sequoyah, then looked back at the audience. "We have all come here today to honor our special hero, Chief Sequoyah!"

While Sequoyah looked on dumbfounded, Ross called for one of the leading chiefs from the Alabama Cherokees to step up beside him and say what he had on his mind.

Chief Grundo moved up beside Ross and paid homage to Chief Sequoyah for the way he had strengthened the Cherokee Nation by giving them their own alphabet and making it possible for them to publish their own books. He called for everyone to stand up and applaud Chief Sequoyah.

The astonished Chief Sequoyah also stood. He wiped tears from his wrinkled cheeks as those around him cheered and applauded.

John Ross had everyone sit down on the ground once again, then said, "I have some very good news for you. Because of Chief Sequoyah's work on the Cherokee language, we are about to have a bilingual newspaper, the *Cherokee Phoenix*, which will be published in Tahlequah. The first edition in Cherokee and in English will come off the press and be distributed all over the Cherokee Nation the first week of October!"

The crowd stood up and applauded and cheered Chief Sequoyah, calling out his name.

When the crowd had once again sat down on the ground, John

Ross called for Pastor Layne Ward to come and tell everyone what was on his heart.

Ward said loud enough for all to hear, "I want to publicly commend Chief Sequoyah for his labor of love in translating the Bible into the Cherokee language. What a blessing it has been to the Cherokee Nation!"

There was much applause and cheering from a good number of people in the crowd.

As Pastor Ward stepped back, voices in the crowd began calling for Chief Sequoyah to speak to them. John Ross smiled at Sequoyah and motioned for him to come where he stood.

The silver-haired Sequoyah rose to his feet, then stepped up beside Ross and faced the crowd. He could not suppress a nervous twitch in his right cheek as he thanked them for the gratitude they had shown him. Tears filled his eyes as he said, "I want you to know that seeing all of my Cherokee friends so happy and satisfied and doing so well in our new homeland means so much to me."

There were more cheers as they applauded his words.

"I want to tell you about something that happened one night in late March, shortly after we North Carolina Cherokees had arrived here in Indian Territory. I was talking with Britt Claiborne—" He stopped and pointed at Britt, who sat with his wife and her family. "He is now *Officer* Britt Claiborne. He and I were discussing how the Cherokee people were already showing signs of being happy in our new homeland. I said to Britt Claiborne that night, 'The stars are bright tonight, aren't they?'

"When Britt Claiborne agreed that the stars were bright, I told him that I believed they were so exceptionally bright because the North Carolina Cherokees were already finding happiness in their new home." A smile spread over Sequoyah's dark features. "And Britt Claiborne agreed with me."

Chief Sequoyah choked slightly, then cleared his throat and said, "With all the happiness around me in the hearts of my Cherokee people, the stars at night really seem to shine with a new brightness!"

The crowd applauded, and once again Chief Sequoyah's eyes sparkled with tears.

n Thursday morning, September 12, Officers Dan Atkins and Britt Claiborne were riding their regular patrol beneath a cloudless sky. About half an hour after they had entered the area owned by the Georgia Cherokees, they topped a steep rise and saw two middle-aged Cherokee farmers on foot some forty yards away. They were talking with a pair of soldiers from Fort Gibson who occupied an army wagon.

"I know those farmers, Britt," Dan said.

One of the Cherokee farmers spotted the two officers and quickly motioned for them to join them. Dan and Britt put their horses to a trot.

"Hello, Erigo…Ulefin," Dan said as they drew up. "Is there a problem here?"

"Yes, Officer Atkins," Ulefin said. "There is a problem."

Both officers dismounted and stepped up to the wagon where the soldiers were seated. Dan introduced himself and Britt to the soldiers, who introduced themselves as Corporal Blake Taylor and Private Marvin McCormick.

"So what's the problem here?" Dan asked.

"I believe you know about two unruly young Seminole men who have caused trouble before," Erigo said. "Their names are Cobra and Python."

"Yes, I know of them. They're brothers, and I've seen them on a few occasions. You've had a problem with them?"

"We have," Ulefin said. "Only a few minutes before these soldiers came along the trail, Erigo and I were riding our horses toward our farms, when Cobra and Python came running out of the woods over there with their rifles pointed at us. They told us to give them our horses or they would kill us and take them."

"We came along shortly after the two horse thieves had ridden away," Corporal Taylor said, "and found Erigo and Ulefin running toward us, all upset. Private McCormick and I were about to go after them, even though we doubted that we could catch them driving this wagon."

"You won't need to go after them now, Corporal," Dan said. "Officer Claiborne and I will chase them down. Which way did they go?"

"That way," Ulefin said, pointing due west.

Dan looked at Britt. "Let's go after them. I know what they look like."

Britt nodded and moved toward his horse. Seconds later, both officers put their horses to a gallop, heading due west across the rolling prairie.

"Have other Seminoles caused trouble in Cherokee territory?" Britt yelled above the sound of the thundering hooves.

"They have, and some Cherokees have done the same to the Seminoles. When the troublemakers are punished, it's under the law of whichever tribe has been offended. Apparently our Cherokee law has not been tough enough on Cobra and Python."

After riding for some twenty minutes, they entered a heavily wooded area, passed through it quickly, and as they emerged on the other side, they saw the two young Seminole Indians off the horses they had stolen, beating an elderly Cherokee man on the ground. He was crying out and trying to defend himself.

"That's them!" Dan shouted.

The Seminoles heard Dan's voice and looked up, then dashed to the stolen horses and grabbed their rifles. The first one to reach his rifle was Cobra. He whirled around while snapping back the hammer, raised the rifle to his shoulder, lined it on Dan Atkins, and fired.

Dan pulled rein just before the slug whistled past his head, nicking his left ear.

Skidding to a halt, Britt pointed his cocked revolver at Python, who was bringing his weapon into play, and yelled, "Drop it!"

Python froze, his eyes bulging, and let his rifle drop to the ground.

Dan aimed his gun at the face of the other Seminole. "Drop it, Cobra!"

As Cobra reluctantly obeyed, Britt noticed the blood trickling from Dan's ear. "Hey, you're bleeding!"

Dan whipped his bandanna from a hip pocket, pressed it to his wounded ear, and said, "Cobra's bullet nicked me."

The brothers were quickly taken into custody. While Dan held them at gunpoint, Britt made them lie facedown on the ground and bound their hands behind their backs and tied their ankles together. Dan told them not to move.

Britt stood over them and glared at them. "Why were you two beating up this old man?"

Cobra and Python looked up at him, but neither replied.

"You're going to be sorry you did this," Britt said, then turned toward the old man.

While the brothers looked on with fear in their eyes, Dan and Britt knelt beside the elderly man, who lay on his back, unconscious.

"I know this man," Dan said. "His name is Aldini. His wife died a few months ago."

Blood was running into the old man's closed eyes from a gash on his forehead. His hair was matted and caked with blood as well. A thin trickle of blood and saliva seeped from his open mouth, soaking his chin and the collar of his buckskin shirt. He was breathing hard, and his lungs were rasping as a low moan escaped his lips.

"Let me see if I can position him so his breathing is easier," Britt said.

"I'll get my canteen," Dan said. "Maybe by pouring some water on that gash on his forehead, I can slow the bleeding."

By making a slight adjustment in Aldini's position, Britt was able to stop the moaning. Britt pulled a bandanna from his hip pocket as Dan came back, canteen in hand, and said, "Go ahead. Pour it on the gash, then I'll tie my bandanna around his head to cover it."

The bleeding slowed once the bandanna had been tied in place, though the gash was still seeping blood.

"We need to get Aldini to Dr. Miles at Fort Gibson, but I don't think he'll be able to endure the ride if we take him on one of our horses. We need a wagon."

Even as the words were coming from Dan's lips, both men heard the sound of hoofbeats and the rattle of a wagon. They turned and saw the army wagon with Corporal Taylor and Private McCormick in the driver's seat and Erigo and Ulefin in the wagon bed behind them.

Both farmers jumped out of the wagon, stared angrily at the two Seminoles on the ground, and ran to their horses, taking hold of the reins. As Taylor and McCormick were getting off the wagon seat, Dan and Britt told them of coming upon the two brothers beating the elderly Cherokee man. Britt explained that Cobra had taken a shot at Dan and nicked his ear.

Still holding the bandanna to his wounded ear, Dan told them that he and Britt were just trying to come up with a way to take Aldini to Dr. Robert Miles at Fort Gibson.

"We'll take him to Dr. Miles," Corporal Taylor said. "We need to be getting back to the fort anyway."

"Great," said Dan, removing the bandanna from his ear and examining it. "We need to get Aldini there as soon as possible."

Britt bent down and cradled the unconscious man in his arms. "I'll put him in the wagon. From the way he's breathing, I think he may have a punctured lung. Those bullies may have broken some of his ribs." Britt eyed the bandanna in Dan's hand. "Is the ear still bleeding?"

Dan shook his head and stuffed the bandanna back in his pocket. "No, it's stopped."

Britt carried Aldini to the rear of the wagon, where Private McCormick had already lowered the tailgate. McCormick hopped into the bed of the wagon and placed himself with his back against one side of the bed. "Just lay him down so I can have his head in my lap, Officer Claiborne."

As Britt did so, Corporal Taylor scrambled up onto the driver's seat.

Britt closed the tailgate, then said, "Private McCormick, that's my bandanna tied around Aldini's head. Try to keep some pressure on that gash, okay?"

"Yes, sir, I will."

Britt thought about how the day had started out warm and sunny, but noted that a cool breeze was now blowing, and Aldini's body was trembling slightly. He stepped up beside the driver's seat. "Just a minute, Corporal. I need to get something to cover our patient with."

Britt hurried to his horse, took a blanket from his saddle pack, and dashed back to the wagon and handed the blanket to Private McCormick.

As soon as the blanket was in place, Taylor said, "We'll get him to Dr. Miles as fast as we can."

Dan nodded. "Officer Claiborne and I work out of the station where Captain Chinando is in charge. Please let us know Aldini's condition as soon as you can."

Britt uttered a prayer for the old man as he watched the wagon disappear over the crest of a small hill.

Erigo and Ulefin stood close by, holding their horses' reins.

When Britt turned around, he saw Dan standing over the Seminoles. His voice was harsh as he said, "I want to know why you two beat up that old man!"

They only looked up at him, but neither would reply.

"You know if he dies, you'll hang, don't you?"

Fear showed in their eyes as the guilty pair looked at each other, but neither said anything.

Dan turned to Britt. "Let's take them to jail."

"Officers, those two horse thieves can ride belly-down on my horse," Erigo said. "Ulefin and I will ride double on his horse."

Dan thanked them, and soon they were on their way toward the station and jail, with Cobra and Python lying side by side over the horse's back.

As they rode at a moderate pace, with Erigo riding behind Ulefin, the two law officers were a few paces ahead of the others.

Britt turned to Dan and said, "I've been pondering the names of our prisoners. I know a little about Seminoles, and I've heard that they often name their male babies after reptiles or fierce animals."

"The greatest Seminole leader when their tribe was in Florida was a warrior named Osceola," Dan said. "Two of Osceola's feisty co-warriors were Alligator and Wild Cat, who stood with Osceola when the U.S. Army went into Florida to take all the Seminoles west to Indian Territory. But Osceola refused to go."

"I've heard and read a little about his refusal to leave Florida."

"Yes, hundreds of Seminole warriors followed him and went to war against the whites. The warriors fled south to the swamps of the Everglades, from which they conducted guerrilla warfare. Osceola was captured after a fierce battle and was taken to the prison at Fort Moultrie, just outside of Charleston. He died in prison shortly afterward."

From their uncomfortable position on Erigo's horse, Cobra and Python glared at the officers with fiery eyes, but remained silent.

At the Claiborne cabin, Cherokee Rose was busily sweeping the floor and dusting the furniture when she paused in her work and ran her gaze over her home. She told herself that even though it was just a small cabin, it was a palace to her.

"It is amazing what being in love can do for a person," she said with a sigh.

As she cleaned and polished the glass lantern chimneys in the parlor, her mind wandered back to the day in North Carolina when she and her parents loaded the family wagon with the few possessions they were allowed to take with them.

"I thought my heart would break into a million pieces when we were forced to say good-bye to our home," she said aloud.

She thought of the journey westward, reliving the horrors and atrocities that were heaped on her people by the cruel soldiers. A shiver ran down her spine.

Just then a ray of sunshine caught her eye as it reflected off the mirror that she and her father had purchased at the general store in Tahlequah before she and Britt had married.

She walked to it, then washed it and began to polish it. As she gave it the last touch with the polishing cloth, she looked at her reflection and said, "The Lord has been so good to you." With that, she bowed her head. "Thank You, dear Lord, for the wonderful blessings that have come to me, even in the midst of great trials and heartaches."

When she looked up again, a happy, radiant image looked back at her from the mirror.

She smiled at her reflection and said, "Cherokee Rose Claiborne, your husband is just going to love what you have to tell him when he comes home this evening!"

At the police station where Dan Atkins and Britt Claiborne were posted, Captain Chinando was sitting at his desk, going over some papers. The window by the desk allowed a clear view of the road that ran by the station, and movement on the road caught his eye. He focused on the horses and riders coming toward the station. Rising from his desk, he hurried out the door, moved up to the riders as they were reining in, and said, "What have we here?"

Dan Atkins and Britt Claiborne dismounted and stepped up to the captain. Between the two of them, they told Chinando the whole story, including that Corporal Blake Taylor and Private Marvin McCormick were rushing the battered, unconscious Aldini to the doctor at Fort Gibson.

Chinando recognized the two Seminoles' names from previous crimes they had committed in Indian Territory. He stepped up to Cobra and Python, who were still belly-down over the horse's back.

"Why did you two beat up on that old man?" he said through his teeth.

Cobra and Python would not so much as look at him.

"You deaf?" Chinando said.

The guilty pair stared at the ground as if the captain did not exist.

After several seconds of silence, Chinando said, "Why did you steal these farmers' horses?"

Silence.

Erigo and Ulefin stepped up close, and Ulefin said to Cobra and Python, "You had better answer the captain! He has the authority to punish you any way he pleases!"

Silence.

Erigo turned to Chinando. "Captain, we want these horse thieves and bullies to be punished to the full extent of the law, even if Aldini lives."

"I assure you, my friends, they *will* be. They will spend many years in the Territory Prison."

The farmers thanked him, then expressed their appreciation to Officers Atkins and Claiborne for capturing the two criminals. With that, they mounted their horses and rode away.

The lawmen took Python and Cobra into the jail and locked them up in separate cells. Both of them sat down on their bunks, faces long, and stared at the floor.

"You two can stare at the floor all you want," Captain Chinando said, "but I know you can hear what I'm saying, so you had better listen. Since these officers caught you in the act of beating Aldini, if he dies, you will hang! I have the authority to hang you!"

Cobra and Python glanced at each other through the bars that separated them, then looked at the captain. Fear showed in their dark eyes, but they said nothing.

Other men in cells around them looked on in silence as Captain Chinando motioned toward the outside door with his chin, and the two officers followed him outside.

"I want to commend both of you for a job well done," the captain. "It's almost lunchtime. Maybe you should eat lunch, then head back to your patrol area."

Dan pulled out his pocket watch and glanced at it. "We can almost make it back to where we left off by noon, Captain. It's best that we head that way."

Chinando smiled. "Whatever works for you is fine. I will see you when you return this afternoon."

The officers mounted their horses, and as they rode away from the station, Britt looked his partner in the eye. "Boy, Dan, I sure am glad your ear stopped bleeding. It had me worried there for a while."

Britt saw tears suddenly fill Dan's eyes.

"Something's bothering you, my friend," Britt said. "Want to talk about it?"

Dan blinked at his tears and cleared his throat. "Since it's almost lunchtime, do you mind if we stop up the road a ways?"

Britt nodded. "Let's pull into that stand of trees up there on the right."

nine

've been wrong, Britt," Dan Atkins said, looking Britt Claiborne square in the eye. "Terribly wrong."

Dan and Britt had ridden their horses into a stand of trees and dismounted.

"What do you mean?" Britt asked.

"You've talked to me over and over about receiving the Lord Jesus as my Saviour. Well, I've been a fool to reject Him." Dan lifted his hand to his ear, which was scabbed with dried blood. "When that bullet nicked my ear and I finally got over the shock if it, I realized just how close I came to being killed. If that rifle slug had been barely more than an inch to the right…" Dan scrubbed a palm over his face, which was now ashen. "I haven't been honest with you, Britt."

"In what way?"

"I told you I wasn't afraid to die. Well, I lied. When that bullet clipped my ear and I realized how close I came to dying, terror gripped me. From what you've shown me in the Bible, I could be in hell right now. Britt, this fool doesn't want to be a fool anymore. I want to be saved."

Tears were glistening in Britt's eyes. "Wait right here, Dan. I'll go get my Bible."

As Britt hurried to his horse, he thanked God for answered prayer. Blackie whinnied at his master as Britt drew up and opened the saddlebag.

"You're happy about this too, eh, Blackie?" he said, taking out his Bible.

Blackie whinnied again and bobbed his head as if he understood what his master was saying.

Britt returned to Dan, and they sat down together on a large rock.

"I've explained God's plan of salvation to you from the Bible several times," Britt said. "But I want to go over it again to make sure you clearly understand. Okay?"

"That's fine. But could I ask you one question before you begin?"

"Of course."

"You told me that hell is a place of literal fire, but I've had other people tell me it isn't so. That there's no fire and torment in hell. Since I trust *you*, I've been scared that if I went to hell, I would burn forever."

Britt opened his Bible. "I'll show you a passage where Jesus told about a man who died and went to hell. If you're willing to take His word on it, that will settle it for you for sure."

When Britt had found the page he wanted, Dan leaned close so he could see it for himself.

"Here in Luke chapter 16, Jesus tells about a rich man who is not saved. He also tells about a poor man, a beggar named Lazarus, who is saved. Look at verse 22: 'And it came to pass, that the beggar died, and was carried by the angels into Abraham's bosom: the rich man also died, and was buried.'

"Abraham's bosom was also called *paradise*. This was where saved people went when they died, before Jesus' resurrection. All right, now let's see where the rich man went. Verses 23 through 24: 'And in hell he lift up his eyes, being in torments, and seeth Abraham afar off and Lazarus in his bosom. And he cried and said, Father Abraham, have mercy on me, and send Lazarus, that he may dip the tip of his finger in water, and cool my tongue; for I am tormented in this flame.' Do you see that? Jesus is quoting this lost man, and he said he was tormented in the *flame*. The last time I checked, Dan, flame was *fire*. Right?"

"Right. Since Jesus said it, I believe it."

"Good. So let's go to some passages about how to miss that awful burning place called hell. First, let's see what God's Word says about the whole human race. Look at Romans 3:23: 'For all have sinned and come short of the glory of God.' All means *all*, doesn't it? *All* of us are sinners."

"That's what the verse says."

"Dan, there are only two ways for human beings to die…in their sins or in Christ. If you die in your sins, you have to go to hell because God will not let even one sin into heaven."

Dan nodded. "Makes sense."

"If you die in Christ, you will go to heaven."

Dan smiled. "That makes sense, too."

"All right," said Britt, flipping pages, "then you have to be *in* Christ to go to heaven. Let's look at John 1:12: 'But as many as received him'—that is, Jesus—'to them gave he power to become the sons of God, even to them that believe on his name.' So those who receive Him are born into God's family, as I told you before, Dan. Remember? 'Except a man be born again, he cannot see the kingdom of God.'"

"I remember. Only those who have been spiritually born into God's family can go to heaven."

"So in order to be born again, you have to *believe* on Jesus' name, which is to believe that He is the one and only Saviour, and you must *receive* Him as *your* Saviour. Dan, are you willing to open your heart to Him?"

Tears filmed Dan's eyes. "I am."

"Okay. Now let me show you something that must go with receiving Jesus into your heart. You must not only tell Him that you are a lost sinner and ask Him to forgive you for all your sins, but you must *repent*. In Luke 13:3, Jesus said, 'Except ye repent, ye shall all likewise perish.' Repentance is a change of mind that results in a change of direction."

Dan was wiping tears. "I understand. I want to receive Him right now."

Britt smiled. "Let's bow our heads, and you call on Him. Tell the Lord Jesus that you know you are a guilty sinner before Him, but you are repenting of your sin and you want to be saved. Ask Him to come into your heart and save you."

After Dan had called on the Lord to save him, Britt prayed for him, asking the Lord to help him to walk close to Him. He then showed Dan some verses from the Bible that offered assurance that he was now saved, and if he died that instant, he would go to heaven. He then showed him in the Bible that his next act of obedience to the Lord was to be baptized. Britt suggested that when their day was over, they go to Pastor Layne Ward. Dan could give the pastor his testimony and ask to be baptized at church next Sunday.

The new convert smiled and agreed. He then thanked Britt for being so patient with him all this time he had been trying to get him to turn to the Lord. Britt told him he just could not give up and that he and Cherokee Rose had been praying for him.

Dan shed tears and expressed his gratitude for Britt and his wife caring so much about where he would spend eternity.

Cherokee Rose was in her kitchen as the sun was lowering below the horizon. She had prepared a special dinner to celebrate the joyous news she was going to share with her husband. The delectable aroma of roast beef, potatoes, carrots, and onions wafted through the cabin. A hint of apple pie with cinnamon filled the air as well.

As dusk began to settle over the plains, Cherokee Rose was concerned that Britt was not home yet. She lit the lanterns in the kitchen, then went through the cabin and lit the rest of the lanterns. With the warm glow of the lanterns all around, she went to the front window and looked outside. A stiff breeze was rustling the colorful fall leaves on the trees near the cabin.

Suddenly, she caught sight of Britt riding Blackie toward the cabin at a fast trot. "Thank You, Lord," she said, her heart pounding as she hurried onto the porch.

"Hello, sweetheart," Britt said as he pulled up and drew rein. "Sorry I'm late."

"I was getting concerned, but it is all right. I am glad you're home safe. Supper is ready."

"Good. I'm hungry. I'll take Blackie to the corral and be right in."

Ten minutes later, when Britt entered the cabin's back door into the kitchen, Cherokee Rose was pouring gravy from a skillet into a bowl. The rest of the food was already on the table.

Britt noted the food on the table and smiled. "Mm-mm! Looks good and smells good, Mrs. Claiborne!"

Britt stepped toward her, and she noticed a glint in his eyes. He took her in his arms, kissed her soundly, then held her at arm's length and said, "I have some very good news for you." Even as he was speaking, he noticed that a strange look had come into his wife's eyes.

"Tell me this good news," she said.

Britt then told her about the young Seminole brothers, Python and Cobra, stealing the Cherokee farmers' horses and how he and Dan pursued them and caught them beating an old Cherokee man named Aldini. He told her how Cobra got off a shot that nicked Dan's ear, but they were able to subdue and capture both Seminoles, who were now locked up in the jail, waiting for sentencing.

Cherokee Rose felt a stabbing pain and lowered her hand to her midsection. Suppressing a gasp that threatened to escape, she took a deep breath and was able to disguise her discomfort. In her heart, she said, *Dear Lord, Britt could have been killed today. Thank You for taking care of him.*

Britt told her how a shook-up Dan Atkins finally got the bleeding on his wounded ear to stop, then told Britt that if the bullet had been an inch to the right, he would have been killed and would have gone to hell.

Cherokee Rose listened with a smile as her husband told her of leading Dan Atkins to the Lord and that the reason he was late getting home was that he took Dan to Pastor Ward, and it was all set for him to be baptized Sunday.

"Oh, darling, this is marvelous!" she said. "I am so glad the Lord answered our prayers and brought Dan to Himself, even if it took some blood from his ear to make it happen. Praise the Lord!"

"Well, now that you know how exciting my day has been, let's eat. I've built up quite an appetite!"

Britt pulled Cherokee Rose's chair out from under the table. As she sat down and he helped her scoot it into place, he said, "Honey, are you all right? You seem sort of lost in thought. Or…or is there a problem I don't know about?"

A silly grin captured Cherokee Rose's face, but she did not reply.

"Okay, Mrs. Claiborne, what is it you're not telling me?" he said, bending down to look her in the eye. "What's the problem?"

"Well…" she said softly, "it is not a problem." She put a hand to her mouth and giggled.

Britt raised his eyebrows. "What are you trying to tell me?"

"You gave me some good news about Dan Atkins getting saved… Well, I have some very good news for you, too!"

He took hold of her hands and looked her square in the eye. "Okay. What is it?"

"I am with child, sweetheart. Our baby will be born in April!"

"Oh, honey, are you sure?"

"Yes. Positive."

Britt's eyes were shining. "A baby of our own! That is more than very good news. That is *wonderful* news!"

He scooted her chair back, picked her up, and whirled her around the kitchen. Suddenly he stopped and carefully set her feet down on the floor. A worried look pinched his features.

"I…I didn't hurt you or the baby, did I?"

"Oh, my, no. Believe me, we are much tougher than that."

Britt folded her into his arms and said, "Thank You, dear heavenly Father, for this wonderful gift. Our first baby. Oh, thank You!"

With tears in his eyes, Britt held her at arm's length again and asked, "Have you told anyone else?"

She shook her head. "I thought you and I should tell my family together. We can tell others later."

Britt sniffed and wiped tears from his cheeks. "Sure. We should tell your family together. Oh, sweetheart, this is so wonderful! It's going to be so exciting to have that baby in our lives, whether it's a boy or a girl."

"Yes, it is, darling." She looked at the cooling food on the table. "We'd better eat. Then we can go tell my father, my grandparents, and my aunt about the baby. I happen to know that they are eating supper together this evening."

"All right, we'll do that." Britt helped Cherokee Rose as she sat down on the chair, then eased onto his own chair. He reached across the table and took hold of her hand. "Sweetheart, we should place our baby into God's hands for His tender care and ask Him to use this child for His glory."

She smiled. "Oh, yes, let us do that."

Cherokee Rose squeezed Britt's hand and whispered her agreement as he spoke to the Lord about the baby. Britt thanked the Lord that once again, out of the depths of adversity, He had blessed them.

There was a knock at the front door of the cabin owned by Chief Bando and Nevarra. "I will see who it is," Bando said as he got up from his chair in the parlor.

Walugo, Tarbee, and Nevarra watched as he opened the door, and all smiled when they saw Britt and Cherokee Rose with the starlit sky behind them. After they all exchanged greetings, Britt said, "Cherokee Rose and I have some good news we want to share with you."

They all sat down, and Britt told the four family members about the happenings that day on the job. Everyone rejoiced when he finished by telling them of leading Dan Atkins to Jesus and that Pastor Ward already had Dan scheduled to be baptized at church on Sunday morning,.

"That certainly is good news!" Walugo said. "Thank you for coming to tell us."

Britt and Cherokee Rose exchanged glances, then Britt said, "Yes, that's good news, but we're not through. I'm going to let my beautiful wife tell you the rest of our exciting news."

All eyes went to Cherokee Rose.

Her eyes sparkled as she said, "I am expecting a baby! If all goes well, our little son or daughter will be born next April!"

Nevarra jumped to her feet. "Oh! Oh! Oh!" She went to her granddaughter and threw her arms around her.

The rest of them converged on the expectant mother, and when all had embraced her and had spoken their joy at the good news, Bando looked at Nevarra and said, "I wonder what it will be like to be married to a great-grandmother."

Nevarra gave him a mock frown. "It will match being married to a great-grandfather!"

Everyone had a good laugh. Then Walugo said, "This is such good news. I cannot help but think how happy Naya would be if she were still here with us."

"I believe that in heaven, the Lord has allowed Naya to learn about the baby," Britt said.

Walugo blinked at the tears that now filled his eyes. "Yes! Yes, of course! You are right, Britt."

Nevarra left her chair and took hold of Cherokee Rose's hand. She glanced out the window toward the night sky and said, "I have to agree with Chief Sequoyah. The stars are bright tonight!"

Walugo brushed tears from his cheeks. "I want to thank the Lord for this wonderful gift and ask Him to protect my daughter and her baby in the months ahead."

All heads were bowed, and Walugo led in the prayer.

he next morning, Britt Claiborne was up before sunrise as usual and stepped out of the cabin while his wife was getting dressed. He went to the small corral to feed Blackie and White Star, and as he poured grain into the feeding trough, he noticed that a bank of fleecy white clouds just above the eastern horizon were turning a rose color. To the south and west, the sky was dark blue, but every minute it grew lighter.

Britt patted the horses' necks as they began to devour the grain, then picked up two buckets and headed for the nearby creek.

By the time he had made three trips to the creek and was pouring the contents of the last bucket into the water trough, the rosy bank of clouds had grown more intense, and soon the sun was blazing out the darkness between the ridges that marked the rolling prairie, giving color to the sweep of the land.

As Britt headed back toward the cabin, he marveled at the beauty of God's sunrise and thanked Him for His creation of the earth.

Officers Britt Claiborne and Dan Atkins entered the police station and greeted Captain Chinando before heading out on patrol. After the captain returned the greeting, Dan said, "Have you heard anything about Aldini?"

Chinando shook his head. "No, not yet. I'm hoping someone from Fort Gibson will come by today and let me know."

Soon Britt and Dan were in their saddles, riding at a moderate trot toward their patrol area.

Dan looked at his partner and said, "Britt, since I asked Jesus to save me, I have such a peace in my heart. It's so good to know that all my sins have been forgiven and that I'm going to heaven whenever it's God's time for me to leave this world."

Britt smiled at him. "I know all about that peace, my friend. I've had it ever since I became a child of God many years ago. I never cease to marvel at the love my Saviour has for me, a sinner who deserves nothing but hell."

Dan nodded. "Just to realize that He loved *me*, Dan Atkins."

"Yes, and *me*, Britt Claiborne. I'll never forget the first time I read Galatians 2:20. Paul wrote of the Son of God who 'loved me, and gave himself for me.' Each one of us can say the same thing. The Son of God loved *me* and gave Himself for *me*!"

"What a Saviour!"

"And the book of Revelation tells us that in the heaven He has prepared for us, 'God shall wipe away all tears from their eyes; and there shall be no more death, neither sorrow, nor crying, neither shall there be any more pain: for the former things are passed away.'"

"I'm so glad you led me to Jesus, Britt."

Britt smiled. "I'm so glad you *let* me lead you to Him, Dan."

That day was without incident, and late in the afternoon as Britt and Dan came riding back to the station to report to Captain Chinando, they saw an army wagon parked in front of the station and the captain talking with two soldiers.

"It's Corporal Taylor and Private McCormick," Britt said.

"Yes!" Dan said. "Let's hurry!"

Less than a minute later, Britt and Dan drew rein, skidding their horses to a halt. The captain and the soldiers were looking at them, their faces drawn, and both Britt and Dan saw a body covered with a blanket in the rear of the wagon.

"Aldini died, didn't he?" Dan said as he and Britt dismounted.

"Yes," Taylor said. "He died while Dr. Miles was trying to save his life."

Captain Chinando stepped up close to his officers. "These men arrived just a few minutes ago. They brought the body back so Aldini's people could have whatever memorial service they wanted and could bury him. I was just telling Corporal Taylor and Private McCormick how to find Aldini's chief."

"Gentlemen, we must be going," Corporal Taylor said. "We'll deliver the body to Aldini's chief, then head back to the fort."

Chinando thanked them for bringing the body back, and as the three lawmen watched the wagon pull away, Chinando said, "Well, I must report Aldini's death to Police Chief Yasson in Tahlequah, and he'll then take the message to the Cherokee General Council. Python and Cobra will be charged with murder, and the Council will set the date for me to hang them."

"They'll make it reasonably soon, won't they?" Britt asked.

"Oh, yes. It won't be long." He took a deep breath. "Well, I need to go and inform those two that they are going to hang." He paused briefly, then said, "Since you two were the arresting officers, I'd like you to be at my side when I tell them."

Dan and Britt followed the captain into the log building that contained the jail cells and noted that both Cobra and Python were now in Cobra's cell and that all the other cells were occupied.

"Appears you've been quite busy, Captain," Britt said.

Chinando nodded. "We were pretty full when this day started, but some of your fellow officers made arrests today. So as you see, I put Cobra and Python in the same cell."

As he spoke, the captain moved toward the cell that held the two killers, with Britt and Dan at his side. Python and Cobra stood at their cell door, looking at them through the bars.

"Python…Cobra…I have news for you," Chinando said. "The old man you beat up has died. Which means you two are going to hang."

Python and Cobra became motionless as stone.

"The date of your execution will be set by the Cherokee General Council," the captain said.

Cobra's flaming eyes darted back and forth between the two officers who had arrested him and his brother.

"Don't look at them like that, Cobra," the captain said. "They were only doing their duty when they arrested you. Blame your-selves that your lives are being cut short. It's your own fault. You took the life of Aldini; now the law will take yours."

The two brothers eyed Britt as he stepped up close and said, "I'd like to talk to both of you about where you're going to go when you die. If you will turn to God's Son, the Lord Jesus Christ, and ask Him to forgive you—"

"I do not want to hear anything about your Jesus Christ!" Cobra shouted. "Leave us alone!"

Britt set his eyes on Python, who growled, "Get away from us, you religious fanatic! We do not want to hear anything you have to say to us!"

Britt held his voice low and level as he said, "Please, at least let me show you from the Bible what God says—"

"Get away from us!" Cobra's features flushed with anger. "We want nothing to do with your Bible!" He turned his back, went to his bunk, and sat down, looking at the floor.

Python did the same.

That evening when Britt Claiborne arrived home, he told Cherokee Rose about Aldini's death and the impending execution of Python and Cobra.

Tears filmed Cherokee Rose's eyes. "It is so sad. Poor Aldini. It was so senseless for those two men to attack him and beat him like they did. From what you have told me, he had nothing for them to steal."

"There was nothing at the scene that belonged to Aldini. They wouldn't tell us why they beat him."

She sniffed and palmed tears from her cheeks. "It's hard to imagine someone so hard-hearted that they would just beat up a helpless old man. They must have no conscience, nor any fear of God."

"Sadly, Satan's evil is all around us in this world. Cobra and Python are perfect examples of that. After Captain Chinando told them they were going to hang, I tried to tell them about the salvation Jesus gives, but they told me in no uncertain terms that they didn't want to hear it."

Cherokee Rose wrapped her arms around her husband, and Britt responded by taking her into his arms.

"Oh, Britt, I am so thankful for the missionaries who came to our village and led my family and me to the Lord."

"And I'm so glad the Lord led the two of us together on that long journey." He took a deep breath and looked down into her tear-fogged eyes. "And now we have a baby coming who will be born into our Christian home."

Cherokee Rose smiled and drew a shaky breath. "I am going to pray for those two young men. Jesus died for them as much as He did for us. I know they did wrong and must suffer the consequences, but just as Jesus saved that thief next to Him on the cross, He is able to save Python and Cobra."

"He most certainly is able, but it's up to them to listen. The thief on the other cross railed at Jesus and would not believe in Him. But I'll try again to get them to listen to the gospel. Let's pray for them right now."

Holding his wife in his strong arms, Britt led as they prayed together for Python and Cobra.

On Sunday, at the close of his sermon, Pastor Layne Ward gave his usual invitation, and three Cherokee teenagers—two girls and a boy—came forward to be saved, and Officer Dan Atkins came forward for baptism. Pastor Ward asked him to tell the congregation how he had come to believe in Jesus Christ as his Saviour, and when he did, there was much rejoicing.

Just then, a middle-aged man named Klippo walked up to Pastor Ward with tears in his eyes and said that he had heard the pastor preach the gospel many times, but it was Officer Atkins's testimony that had caused him to see what a fool he was to keep rejecting Christ. At the pastor's request, Britt Claiborne took Klippo to the side and led him to the Lord.

The congregation then followed Pastor Ward to the nearby creek, and Dan Atkins, Klippo, and the three teenagers were baptized.

On the way home after the service, Britt and Cherokee Rose had a wonderful time praising the Lord together. They also talked about the baby in her womb and rejoiced again in the precious gift the Lord had given them.

On Monday morning, before Dan and Britt left the police station to ride their patrol, Britt told Dan that he wanted to try once again to get Python and Cobra to listen to the gospel. Dan went with him, and when they stepped up to the cell where the brothers were seated on their bunks, the condemned men saw the Bible in Britt's hand.

Python jumped to his feet, eyes bulging, and screamed, "Get out of here! We already told you we do not want to hear what you have to say!"

Cobra was at his brother's side. "We hate you, Claiborne!" he shouted as loud as he could. "And we hate your partner, too!"

The other prisoners looked on through the bars of their cells, eyes wide.

Suddenly the door of the log building opened, and Captain Chinando entered, a frown on his face. "What is going on in here?"

Cobra hissed through his teeth, "This Claiborne man of yours is trying to force his religion on us! We do not want to hear it! Make him and his partner leave us alone!"

The captain looked at Britt and Dan. "Let's go outside."

They left, and as the three of them walked toward the station building where Britt's and Dan's horses were tied, the captain said, "I'm glad you care about those two killers, Britt, but as you can see, they're not going to listen to you. It's best that you not rile them anymore."

"All I could do was try, Captain," Britt said.

On the following Monday morning, September 18, Chief John Ross was working around his cabin when he saw two riders, both well-dressed Cherokee men, draw up.

"Good morning," John said. "Is there something I can do for you?"

"We are from the Cherokee General Council headquarters in Tahlequah, Chief John Ross," said the man whose horse was closest to him. "My name is Waynoni, and my partner, here, is Comando. May we talk to you?"

"Of course," John said. "Please come into my cabin."

When they were seated in the parlor area of John's cabin, Waynoni said, "The General Council held an important meeting yesterday, Chief John Ross. All of the Council members know who you are and what you have done for the Cherokee Nation over the years. Comando and I have been sent to ask if you will return with us and meet with the Council on some important matters. This is all we can tell you at this point, but you will learn what the meeting is all about when you attend it."

"I will be glad to go with you. I will saddle my horse, then I will need to let a couple of the chiefs close by know where I am going."

Not long after, John mounted his horse, and the three of them rode northeastward across the rolling prairie. Waynoni and Comando asked many questions about John Ross's years of service to the Cherokee Nation in North Carolina, Tennessee, Georgia, and Alabama, and about the long journey from North Carolina to Indian Territory. When they learned that his wife, Quatie, was one of some four thousand who had died on the Trail of Tears, they both spoke their condolences.

Waynoni and Comando told John Ross that they had heard how cruel the soldiers were to the Indians and asked if this was true.

"Yes, I am afraid it is true," John said. "But let me also tell you of one soldier who was very kind to our people…Lieutenant Britt Claiborne, who himself is a quarter Cherokee. Many, many times on the journey, Lieutenant Claiborne protected us from the cruelty of the soldiers. At times, he even had to use his fists to do so."

"Good for Lieutenant Britt Claiborne," said Waynoni, nodding.

"Lieutenant Claiborne is now an officer on the Indian Territory Police Force and has married the granddaughter of Chief Bando."

Comando smiled. "I have heard of Chief Bando. I am pleased that Officer Claiborne is married to his granddaughter."

Comando then said that the soldiers of Fort Gibson were not cruel to the Indians, but had shown themselves to be their friends.

"Yes, I have seen this," John said, "especially when the soldiers were helping the North Carolina Cherokees build their cabins."

"I am so glad for Dr. Robert Miles at the fort," Waynoni said. "He gladly cares for Indians who are sick or injured when they are brought to him."

John Ross nodded. "I have heard this about Dr. Miles, and I deeply appreciate his kindness and compassion toward our people."

The three men continued to converse as they rode. They were just a few miles from Fort Gibson and were riding alongside a bubbling stream. Suddenly, a rattlesnake appeared, coiling and hissing from a low spot right in front of Waynoni's horse. Waynoni's horse violently shied and leaped sideways, and Waynoni was thrown from the saddle and landed on the hard ground.

Comando and John Ross quickly dismounted, and while Comando rushed to Waynoni, Ross picked up a large round rock and rolled it hard toward the hissing reptile. The snake did exactly as Ross had expected it to. It made a strike at the oncoming rock, and when the snake and the rock collided, the snake's head was shattered.

eleven

hen Chief John Ross saw the rattlesnake's head shatter, he wheeled and dashed to the fallen Waynoni, where Comando was kneeling beside him. Concern showed on John's face as he knelt beside Comando and looked into Waynoni's pain-filled eyes. "Are you hurt bad, Waynoni?"

"His right leg is broken," Comando said. "See?"

Comando had lifted the right pant leg, and John Ross saw the protruding sharp point of bone under the skin.

"We must get him to Dr. Miles at Fort Gibson," Comando said.

Ross rose to his feet. "Yes, as soon as possible. We need to make a splint for his leg. I'll go over to that wooded area and break off a couple of slender tree limbs to make the splint."

Comando stood up and drew his long knife from its sheath. "I will help you. Waynoni, we will be right back."

Gritting his teeth, Waynoni nodded.

As Ross and Comando were moving toward the nearby wooded area, Comando said, "I saw you kill that rattlesnake by rolling that stone at it. That was a smart thing to do!"

"I learned that when I was a boy," John said. "Rattlesnakes will strike at anything that appears to threaten them. We had plenty of rattlers on our farm, and my father taught me how to kill them by rolling good-sized stones at them. It never fails."

They drew up to a stand of cottonwood trees, and John looked them over.

"This one over here has some low-hanging limbs that should be just about right, Comando."

Comando reached up, took hold of a limb, and snapped it at the trunk, then used his knife to cut through the waxy bark. He handed it to John, then did the same thing with another limb about the same size and length.

When they walked back to where Waynoni lay on the ground, John said, "It may hurt you some when we tie these limbs to your leg, Waynoni, but the splint will hold the broken bone in place while we ride to the fort. It would hurt a whole lot more if we didn't splint it."

"I am sure you are right, Chief John Ross," Waynoni said through gritted teeth.

"I happen to have some rawhide strips in my saddlebags, Comando," Ross said. "I'll be right back."

A few minutes later, Waynoni tried his best to keep from crying out while Ross and Comando were lining up the tree limbs on either side of his broken leg and lashing them together with the rawhide strips. He ground his teeth and ejected a few moans, but didn't cry out in pain.

"All right, Comando," John Ross said, "let's put him in the saddle on my horse. I'll sit behind him, and you can lead his horse as we ride."

With one man on each side of Waynoni, they picked him up and carefully hoisted him into the saddle on John's horse. A small groan escaped his tightly pressed lips. His splinted leg stuck out at an odd angle.

John Ross quickly mounted up behind Waynoni, took hold of the reins, and they headed toward the fort.

John laid a hand gently on the injured man's shoulder. "You doing all right, my friend?"

Waynoni turned his head slightly and gave him a weak smile. "I am doing all right. But I will be very glad when this ride is over."

"Can't blame you for that. Just try to relax, and we will have you to Dr. Miles in a short time."

It was early afternoon when John Ross and Comando rode up to the front gate of Fort Gibson. The two guards at the gate were kind to them when Comando explained who they were and what had happened to Waynoni. One of the guards called to a lieutenant who was passing by to come and lead them to Dr. Miles's office.

Lieutenant Wade Henderson led them up to the front of the office. As Ross and Comando were carefully easing Waynoni down from the saddle, Henderson said, "I will go to General Danford and let him know what has happened and that Chief John Ross is here."

"Yes, please do that," Comando said.

Before Ross and Comando reached the door of the doctor's office with Waynoni in their arms, the door came open, and a woman in a dark blue dress and white pinafore apron said, "Please come in, gentlemen. It looks like you have a man with a broken leg here."

"Yes, ma'am," Comando said. "His name is Waynoni. He and I are with the Cherokee General Council, and this man with us is Chief John Ross. Is Dr. Miles here?"

"He is," she said as they carried Waynoni through the door. "I'm his daughter and his nurse. My name is Mary Stapler." She set her soft blue eyes on Ross. "I have heard much about you, Chief. It is an honor to meet you."

John smiled. "Thank you, ma'am."

She gestured toward a wooden chair. "Please place Waynoni here on this chair. I'll go get my father. He's mixing medicine in the back room."

When Dr. Robert Miles returned with his daughter, Comando explained the situation to them.

Dr. Miles shook hands with Chief John Ross, saying that he had heard much of his leadership work with the Cherokee Nation and that it was an honor to meet him. He then asked Ross and Comando to carry the injured man to the back room, where he would examine his leg.

John Ross was impressed with Dr. Miles and also with his daughter as they removed the crude splint and examined Waynoni's broken leg. The doctor then asked that they go to the front of the office and wait while Waynoni's leg was being set.

Ross and Comando had just sat down in the waiting area when

General Austin Danford came through the door and welcomed them. He had never met Comando, but brought up the time he spent with Chief John Ross when the North Carolina Cherokees first arrived at the fort after their long journey.

Danford and Ross talked about that time for a moment. Then the general said, "Lieutenant Henderson told me why you are here, Chief. I figured I would be seeing you soon."

"Oh?"

"A few days ago I was talking with some of the members of the Council while I was in Tahlequah. They told me that they expected the day would come soon when the Council would be contacting you about some very important business. They didn't say what the business was, but emphasized that it was indicative of notable worth."

John smiled. "Oh, really? Well, I do not know what it is either, but I am eager to find out."

"Well, will you do me a favor, Chief?" the general said.

"Of course."

"Will you stop by the fort after you've met with the Council and let me know what it's all about?"

"I certainly will."

Soon, Mary Stapler came out of the back room, and John and Comando stood to their feet.

"I'm happy to tell you that Waynoni's leg has been set without any complications, and the doctor is now putting it in a cast. He asked, Comando, that you come into the back room so he can talk to you about the care Waynoni is going to need when he gets back home to Tahlequah."

"Yes, ma'am," Comando said and headed for the back room.

Mary sat down at her desk and pointed to a chair in front of the desk. "Please sit down, Chief Ross."

John eased onto the chair, and she leaned toward him, putting her elbows on the top of the desk. "I've heard many horrible stories about the awful journey you and your Cherokee people were forced to make from North Carolina. I understand you were their leader on the journey."

John nodded. "Yes, ma'am."

"I understand the soldiers who brought all of you here were quite cruel."

"Yes, ma'am. Not all of them, but most of them were."

"My husband was a soldier," Mary said with a sad note in her voice. "He was killed in a battle with the Ponca Indians in Kansas six years ago. But I can assure you that if he had been on your journey, he would never have been cruel to you and your people. Duane was a brave and diligent soldier, Chief, but he was also a man of compassion."

John saw the anguish in Mary's eyes as she spoke of her husband. "I'm sure he was, ma'am. Comando told me before we arrived here that your husband had been killed in battle a few years ago. It must have been very difficult for you to be made a widow at such a young age."

Mary bit down on her lower lip. "Yes. I was thirty-seven at the time. It was very difficult indeed. If I hadn't had the Lord to help me in my deep sorrow, I don't know what I would've done."

John had noticed the Bible that lay on Mary's desk. "There is nothing like having the God of heaven to help us when we are in dire need, that's for sure. But I am so sorry your husband was killed, ma'am. Do you have children?"

She shook her head. "No. I'm not able to bear children."

"I can sympathize with you in losing your mate, ma'am. I will be forty-nine in October. My wife, Quatie, died on the journey from North Carolina."

"Oh, I am so sorry. Then you can indeed sympathize with me. From all I've heard about that ordeal, I'm surprised that any of you made it."

"It was only by the grace of God that we did, Mrs. Stapler. We are thankful to have finally found a place to call home again."

"I'm sure you are."

"My pastor preached about our new home a few weeks ago, then took us to Ecclesiastes, where God speaks of man going to his *long home* when he dies. To those Cherokees who know Christ as Saviour, Pastor Ward said that when we go to our heavenly home, no one can ever make us move again. We will abide there forever."

A smile spread over Mary's face. "Amen!"

John matched her smile. "So you know the Lord Jesus as your Saviour."

"He saved me when I was ten years old."

"I was also ten when I received Him into my heart."

"Well, we have much in common then, don't we?"

"Yes, ma'am, we do."

"Speaking of *home*, I have moved many times in my life. When I was a child, we moved quite often with my father being a military physician. Then with my husband in the army, we moved from fort to fort many times. The word *home* has such a special meaning to me, and as the saying goes, 'There's no place like home.'"

At that moment, Dr. Miles came into the office, pushing a wheelchair with a half-conscious Waynoni in it and Comando following. A cast was on Waynoni's right leg.

"Chief Ross," the doctor said, "we have an army wagon on its way to carry Waynoni to Tahlequah. Riding on a horse would be too difficult. Comando will be bringing Waynoni back for me to check on his leg within a week. I'll keep a close check on him until I can remove the cast."

"I appreciate your kindness to him, Doctor," John said.

They heard hoofbeats and the sound of a wagon rattling. They looked out the front window and saw an army wagon pull up and stop in front of the office, with two soldiers on the seat.

Comando opened the door, and Dr. Miles pushed the wheelchair out to the wagon. Comando followed and helped one of the soldiers place Waynoni in the rear of the wagon. Dr. Miles took a bottle from one of the pockets of his white coat and handed it to Waynoni, giving him instructions on taking the medicine.

At the same time, Mary Stapler said to John, "Chief Ross, will you stop by the fort on your way back home from Tahlequah? My mother died a few years ago, so I cook all of Daddy's meals for him. I'd like for you to share a meal with Daddy and me."

"Nothing has been said about my staying overnight in Tahlequah, so I assume the meeting will be over sometime this afternoon. If that is so, I will gladly eat supper with you and your father this evening."

Mary's eyes glittered and she smiled. "All right. I will look forward to it."

John found her smile captivating. "So will I, ma'am. Thank you."

John stepped outside, moved up to the side of the wagon, and looked at the groggy Waynoni lying in the wagon bed. One of the soldiers climbed in to sit beside him. The other soldier tied Waynoni's horse to the rear of the wagon, then made his way onto the driver's seat and took the reins in hand.

Comando and Chief John Ross mounted their horses. As they pulled out, John looked back and saw Mary at the medical office door. She smiled and waved to him, and John waved back.

❦

Cherokee Rose had prepared lunch for her father and her grandparents. As Walugo, Bando, and Nevarra were taking their places
at the table in Cherokee Rose's bright kitchen, the hostess placed
the last food item on the table—a steaming platter of venison
stew—and started to sit down in her chair. Suddenly, she covered
her mouth and said between her fingers, "Please excuse me." Even
as she spoke, Cherokee Rose dashed to the back door and stepped
outside.

At the table, Nevarra rose from her chair. "I think it is 'morning sickness' at noon," she said to the two men. "Go ahead and
start eating." With that, she headed for the door.

Walugo and Chief Bando stared after her in silence.

Outside, Nevarra saw her granddaughter off the porch, grasp-
ing the railing as she bent over. Nevarra stepped down onto the
ground and moved up to her. Cherokee Rose straightened up and
looked at her grandmother, her face ashen and her body trembling.

Nevarra embraced her. "Are you all right, little one?"

Cherokee Rose leaned into her grandmother's arms and took
a deep, cleansing breath. "I am all right, for the moment anyhow.
This has always been happening first thing in the morning. It did
not today, so I thought maybe I was through with this phase. But
when I smelled that venison stew as I put it on the table, it just
overpowered me."

"Well, honey, do not worry about it," Nevarra said. "You will
soon be beyond this part of it, and you will begin feeling better.
You may find yourself tiring easily as the months pass and wanting
to sleep a good deal. But that is God's way of caring for you and the
baby. Your body will go through some unusual changes, but when

the day comes that you hold that precious baby in your arms, it will all be worth it!"

"I know it will be. It is all so strange and new to me, but each day is so exciting. Preparing for our wee one makes each day so special."

A cool breeze was blowing, and Cherokee Rose was shivering. Nevarra hurried her back into the kitchen. Walugo and Bando looked up from the table as the women entered, a knowing look passing between them.

"How about a nice cup of hot tea and some bread and butter instead of venison stew?" Nevarra said to Cherokee Rose.

"That does sound good, Grandmother. Thank you."

"I have been where you are, child, and a strong cup of tea always helped me."

As grandmother and granddaughter smiled at each other, the bond between them grew stronger.

While Cherokee Rose ate bread and drank tea, the others enjoyed the venison stew.

"I saw Chief John Ross and two well-dressed Cherokee strangers at the front of his cabin early this morning," Walugo said. "I am wondering who the strangers were. Did you happen to see them, Bando?"

"I did. John brought them to our cabin to let me know they were members of the Cherokee General Council and that they had asked him if he would go with them to Tahlequah to meet with the Council on important business."

"Did John tell you what the business was?"

"He told me that he would not learn what it was until he got to the meeting, but he was sure it must be important. He came to our cabin simply to let me know where he would be all day. I think the Council just may want John to help with something important to the Cherokee government."

"You are probably right, Grandfather," said Cherokee Rose, whose face was losing its pale cast. "We all know that the best man for any governing task in the Cherokee Nation is Chief John Ross."

twelve

hief John Ross arrived in Tahlequah with Comando riding beside him and the wagon carrying Waynoni just behind them. Comando hipped around in his saddle and said to the soldiers in the wagon, "I will take Chief John Ross to the Cherokee General Council building. Then I will catch up with you as you head toward Waynoni's house. How is he doing?"

"He's asleep!" called out the soldier in the wagon bed.

"That is good! Sleep will help him."

They came to the town's main intersection and turned left. After a short distance, they hauled up to the front of an impressive brick building, with twin towers pointing skyward above the front door and a large sign that read:

CHEROKEE GENERAL COUNCIL OFFICES
AND MEETING HALL

"I like the looks of this place, Comando," John said as he ran his gaze over the well-built structure.

"Most everyone who sees it for the first time is impressed, Chief."

They dismounted and tied their horses' reins to the hitch rail, then headed for the front door.

"You will like Thundro, our Council chairman," Comando said. "He is a full-blooded Cherokee. Like you, he holds the Cherokee Nation in high esteem and has devoted his life to serving our people."

Comando opened the door and gestured for John to enter, then led him down the first hall they came to. The first door they approached had a sign in English and Cherokee that announced it was Thundro's office.

Comando opened the office door, and John noted a young Cherokee man sitting at a desk behind a waist-high counter. The young man, who was well-dressed like Waynoni and Comando, greeted Comando by name, then rose to his feet with a smile. "This must be Chief John Ross."

"It certainly is," Comando said. "Chief John Ross, meet Yondini, Thundro's secretary."

"Chairman Thundro is expecting you," Yondini said. "I will tell him that you are here."

Before Yondini reached the door of the inner office, it came open, and a stout, well-dressed Cherokee man filled the frame-work. He smiled. "Ahh! Comando has brought Chief John Ross to me as planned."

Comando introduced the chairman and the chief, then Thundro said, "Where is Waynoni?"

Comando told Thundro about the rattlesnake and Waynoni's fall from the horse and that Dr. Robert Miles at Fort Gibson had treated him.

"I am sorry about Waynoni's misfortune," Thundro said. "I trust that he will be all right."

"Dr. Miles expects Waynoni to heal up in time and be fine," Ross said.

"Good. Well, I will now send messengers to all the Council members to let them know that you are here, Chief John Ross. We will gather in just over an hour…at three o'clock."

At three o'clock in the meeting hall, Chairman Thundro presented Chief John Ross to the fifty-six men of the Cherokee General Council as the two of them stood together on the platform.

All the councilmen rose from their seats, applauding Ross and shouting words of welcome.

When the applause and shouting died down, the chairman looked at Ross and said, "I want to commend you, Chief John Ross, for all that you have done for the North Carolina Cherokees over the years, and what you did for the entire Cherokee Nation when you were president of the National Council of Cherokees." Thundro then laid a hand on Ross's shoulder. "And now, my friend, I want to get down to why we have asked you to come here today."

John smiled and nodded.

"The Council plans to establish what we are going to call the United Cherokee Nation. Because of the confidence we have in the leadership you have displayed over these many years, and because of your wholehearted devotion to the Cherokee people, we have invited you to this meeting to ask a favor of you. We want you to write the constitution for our new government."

"Mr. Chairman, I am deeply touched and greatly honored by the Council's confidence in me," John Ross said. "And yes, I will be glad to write the constitution for the new United Cherokee Nation!"

The councilmen rose to their feet, applauding, and Thundro applauded where he stood. When the applause faded and the councilmen sat down again, John Ross said, "I will go to work on it immediately upon my arrival back home, and when it is finished, I will return with the constitution for the Council's approval. I estimate that it will take me about a week to write it, since I am familiar with constitutions from my past experience."

"We will wait for your return, Chief John Ross," Thundro said. "I very much appreciate your willingness to do this for us."

After Thundro dismissed the meeting, Chief John Ross mounted his horse and rode to Fort Gibson. There he reported to General Austin Danford about why the Cherokee General Council had asked to meet with him, and General Danford voiced his approval. Then John led his horse across the fort's complex to the medical office. He tied the reins to the hitch rail and entered the building.

Mary Stapler was at her desk, and when she looked up, her eyes brightened and a smile curved her lips. She rose to her feet and said, "Hello, Chief Ross. I assume the meeting is over."

"Yes, ma'am. I just left the Council headquarters and stopped to see General Danford for a few minutes. And now, here I am as promised and looking forward to enjoying your cooking."

She blushed. "Well, I hope it lives up to your expectations. I'll be leaving for the house in a few minutes to start dinner. So what was the business the Council wanted with you?"

Dr. Robert Miles entered the office from the rear of the building, talking to a soldier he had just treated, and said, "Hello, Chief Ross."

"Hello, Doctor."

Miles turned to the soldier. "Be sure to come back in three days and let me check you."

The soldier nodded. "I certainly will, Doctor." He looked at Mary. "Thank you for your help, Mrs. Stapler."

"My pleasure," she said. "See you Saturday."

When the soldier was gone, Dr. Miles said, "Chief, I heard Mary asking you what the business was that the Council wanted with you. We'd both like to hear it. Let's sit down, and you tell us all about it."

The three of them sat on chairs in the waiting area, and when father and daughter had heard the purpose of the meeting, they both congratulated John for the confidence the Council had shown in him.

Mary then said, "Daddy, John is eating with us this evening, so since we have no one else coming in today as far as we know, I'll go home and get dinner started."

At the Miles house, Mary Stapler worked quickly to prepare the evening meal. She had put a chicken in the oven to roast when she was home at noon, and when the doctor and John Ross entered the house a few minutes after five, they commented to each other on how good dinner smelled.

As Dr. Miles closed the door behind them, John looked around the parlor. A fire was crackling in the fireplace, and lamps were burning, giving the room a cozy look.

Mary came rushing in from the hall that led to the kitchen. "Dinner is ready in the dining room, gentlemen. Better get your hands washed."

The doctor looked at the chief. "Let's go wash up. Follow me."

Soon they were seated at the dining room table, where lighted candles gleamed on the snowy white tablecloth.

"What a lovely home," John said as he gazed around the room.

The doctor smiled. "My daughter has completely redecorated the house since my wife died. My wife kept it looking nice, but my daughter has a touch that amazes me."

The doctor asked John Ross to pray over the food, then they began to eat. When the main course was finished, they lingered for some time, taking pleasure in warm apple pie and coffee.

When they were finally finished, John smiled at Mary. "It's been a long time since I have enjoyed such a fine meal, ma'am. You are a great cook."

A rosy stain appeared on Mary's cheeks. "Thank you, Chief. Daddy and I are so glad you could share it with us."

"You must come and eat with us again sometime soon," the doctor said.

Mary smiled happily at both men, then said, "Please make it *very* soon, Chief."

"I will, ma'am, but only if you call me John from now on."

"Well, only if you change the *ma'am* to *Mary* from now on."

"All right, Mary, it's a deal! I will be back through here in a week or so with the new constitution for the Council to read and hopefully accept."

The doctor nodded. "All right. When you come back, you must have another meal with us. Just come to the office or here to the house, depending on what time of day it is."

Mary's blue eyes sparkled. "Yes, John. The invitation stands."

"Neither of you has to twist my arm, I guarantee you," John said.

Later that night, as John entered his cabin and readied himself for bed, he could not get the image of Mary Stapler from his mind. "She is such a delightful Christian lady," he said to himself as he pulled back the covers. "I feel so comfortable around her."

At Fort Gibson, Mary extinguished the lantern on the small table beside her bed and snuggled down under the covers. "Lord, such a wonderful, unselfish man as John Ross shouldn't have to live the rest of his life alone."

Before sunrise on Thursday morning, September 26, John Ross mounted up and rode from his home in the North Carolina Cherokee area of Indian Territory toward Tahlequah. In his saddle-bags were two copies of the constitution he had written for the new United Cherokee Nation.

When he reached Fort Gibson, he spent a few minutes with General Austin Danford, then rode to the medical office. It was a few minutes after eight o'clock.

Dr. Robert Miles came out the door, medical bag in hand, as John was dismounting. "Hello, Chief," he said warmly. "I'm on my way to deliver a baby for the wife of one of the fort's officers. You must have finished the constitution."

"Yes, sir."

"Well, I'm sure the Council will like it." With that, the doctor hurried away.

John opened the door, and Mary was just coming into the office from the rear of the building as he stepped through the doorway. She charmed him again with her enchanting smile as she hurried toward him.

"Good morning, John!" she said. "This must be constitution day!"

"It sure is. So I thought I would just do as I was told and announce my presence so I could have another one of those scrumptious meals."

"Well, you will probably be pretty busy most of the day, so how about dinner again?"

"That will be great! I'll come here to the office if I am free by four o'clock. Otherwise, I will come to the house and do my best to be there no later than six. Okay?"

"Sounds good to me."

John got the same smile from Mary just before he went out the door. He felt the warmth of it lingering in his heart as he rode the short distance to Tahlequah.

Cherokee General Council chairman Thundro looked up from his desk to see Chief John Ross entering his office. He smiled, hurried to him, and shook his hand. "Do you have the constitution finished?" he asked, with excitement showing in his eyes.

"Yes, sir," said John, handing him the two copies of the proposed constitution.

"Well, come sit down in this chair that faces my desk while I read it."

John watched Thundro's eyes as he read the important document. When the chairman was finished, he said, "Chief John Ross, it is perfect! There is not one thing I would want to change."

Messengers were sent to advise the Council members that Chief John Ross was back in Tahlequah with the proposed constitution and that they were to meet at ten o'clock that morning.

At ten o'clock, all the Council members were present in the meeting hall, including Waynoni, who was now on crutches and told John Ross he was doing quite well.

Chairman Thundro stood before the Councilmen and read the constitution aloud to them, making comments as he went along as to how much he liked the way certain important matters were worded. When he finished, he asked if anyone had questions or had heard anything they wished to change.

There were no questions and not one negative comment. Chairman Thundro commended Ross for the well-written constitution, and a vote was taken. The constitution was accepted by all.

When the meeting was dismissed, every man of the Council took time to go to Chief John Ross and commend him for a job well done.

After lunch with Waynoni, Comando, and Thundro at a café that had just opened up in Tahlequah, John mounted his horse and rode toward Fort Gibson. He presented himself at the front gate for a second time that day and was welcomed by the guards.

When he stepped into the medical office, it was just past three thirty. Mary and her father were standing at her desk, and they greeted him with smiles.

"I have a feeling the Council accepted your work with pleasure," Dr. Miles said.

"Yes, sir. They accepted it exactly as I wrote it."

"Excellent, though I'm not surprised," the doctor said. "You *will* be dining with us this evening?"

"I will."

"Good. Well, I must get back to my patient. You and Mary sit down and chat for a while."

John looked at Mary, then met her father's gaze. "We will just do that, Doctor."

Thirteen

n Tahlequah on Tuesday, October 1, the Cherokee General Council gathered in the meeting hall. When everyone was seated, Chairman Thundro stood before them and said, "Gentlemen, as you know, one of our duties during our regular monthly meeting is to discuss crimes committed in Indian Territory during the previous month. It is our responsibility to consider the crime or crimes and to pronounce sentence upon those who committed them."

Thundro gestured toward the man sitting in a chair on the platform just behind him. "Also with us for this meeting is our Indian Territory police chief, Yasson, whose office is here in Tahlequah."

Chairman Thundro then read the crime reports, one by one, from the month of September. As each man's crime or crimes were presented, Thundro answered any questions from the councilmen, and after some discussion, they came to an agreement on how long the guilty man should be sentenced to the Territory Prison located just outside of Tahlequah.

After almost three hours, when the decisions had been made and recorded, the chairman ran his gaze over the faces of the councilmen and said, "I have held the one capital crime committed in the Territory for last."

He then brought up the two Seminole Indians, Python and Cobra, who were being held in the jail under Captain Chinando's command. He pointed out that they had beaten an old Cherokee man named Aldini and were caught in the very act by Officers Dan Atkins and Britt Claiborne, arrested, and jailed.

Thundro cleared his throat. "Aldini was brought to Dr. Robert Miles at Fort Gibson for treatment of his wounds, but he died while Dr. Miles was trying to save his life." Thundro set his jaw. "Their crime, therefore, was murder. This report from Captain Chinando says that neither Python nor Cobra has shown any remorse for what they did."

Police Chief Yasson stepped up beside Thundro and said so all could hear, "The law in Indian Territory says that those murderers are to be hanged. I suggest, Chairman Thundro, that the sentence be carried out soon."

"I agree, Chief Yasson." Thundro looked to the councilmen and said, "If you are in agreement that the guilty pair are to be hanged as our law prescribes, please stand."

Within a few seconds, every man was on his feet.

Thundro nodded. "All right. It is unanimous." He looked at a small calendar he had lying on the speaker's desk. Then looking up, he said, "I suggest we set this coming Thursday, October 3, as the day of execution. Everyone in favor, please stand."

Again, every councilman stood.

Late that afternoon, Officers Dan Atkins and Britt Claiborne were riding toward the station after their day on patrol, ready to give their report. Dan's spiritual hunger had him asking Britt Bible questions, and Britt adeptly answered him.

Soon they drew up to the station, and as they were dismounting, they saw three riders coming their direction.

"Those men are in police uniforms," Britt said. "I recognize Chief Yasson. Do you know the other two?"

"Officers Sadro and Melidan, who serve under Chief Yasson in Tahlequah. I'm sure they're here to give the sentencing report to Captain Chinando from the General Council. Chief Yasson doesn't usually come to make the report. It must be because Python and Cobra have been given the death sentence."

As the three riders drew up, Chief Yasson said, "Hello, Officers Atkins and Claiborne. Just get in from your patrol?"

"Yes, sir," Dan said. "We're about to give Captain Chinando our report for the day."

The police chief and his two officers dismounted. Chief Yasson introduced them to Britt Claiborne, then took a large envelope out of his saddlebag.

"I want to commend you two men for catching Python and Cobra," Yasson said. "The Cherokee General Council has set the day after tomorrow for them to be hanged. I am here to give the official papers to Captain Chinando for this and for the sentencing of the other men in your jail to the Territory Prison."

As Dan and Britt led the Tahlequah policemen through the door of the station, Captain Chinando was just coming in the rear door from the jail building. With him was a young Cherokee man in uniform. Captain Chinando greeted the chief and his men, then introduced the young man, saying his name was Roxudi.

"I have just hired Roxudi to work here as my assistant. He has only a little experience in law enforcement over at one of the Georgia Cherokee jails, but comes highly recommended. I need an assistant to be right here, especially when I have to be away from my office."

Yasson smiled. "Well, Captain, I am sure that with you training him, Roxudi will become quite proficient."

Chinando rubbed his jaw and said, "I assume you are here with the sentencing information from today's meeting of the General Council."

Yasson lifted the envelope and handed it to him. "You will find your information in here, Captain. I will tell you now that the Council has set this Thursday, October 3, as the date for Python and Cobra to be hanged. The rest of your prisoners will be picked up by an army wagon and taken to the Territory Prison in a few more days. Probably Friday or Saturday."

"Chief, I'd like for you to come into the jail and tell Python and Cobra that they will be hanged on Thursday for their crime. It would be good for them to hear it from you."

Yasson nodded. "I am willing to do that."

When Chief Yasson and his men entered the jail building with Captain Chinando and Officers Atkins and Claiborne, they took note that the cells were all occupied. Some had two prisoners in them, and others had one. Chinando stepped up to a cell and told the two men inside that Chief of Police Yasson from Tahlequah was there and had a message for them.

Both Seminoles stepped up close to the barred door and gave Yasson a rancorous look.

Yasson ran his gaze between them and said, "Which of you is Python and which one is Cobra?"

"Why don't you take a guess?" Python said.

Chinando pointed to them and said, "This one is Python and this one is Cobra. Go ahead, Chief Yasson. Tell them."

Yasson's jaw squared as he looked them in the eye. "You two should be ashamed of yourselves for beating up that old man and causing his death. The Cherokee General Council has given Captain Chinando the authority to hang you the day after tomorrow."

"At sunrise," Chinando added.

Both killers glared at Chinando and Yasson with hate-filled eyes, then directed their glare to the two officers who had arrested them.

Britt stepped up closer. "Don't look at us like that. It's *your* fault that you're going to be hanged, not ours."

"Well, men, the message has been delivered," Chinando said. "We can go now."

As the men turned to leave, Yasson asked Britt and Dan what area they covered on their daily patrol. While they slowly walked toward the outer door, Dan described their route, giving some landmarks.

Python and Cobra listened intently, then heard Yasson say, "Captain Chinando, you are to bury Python and Cobra in that same field over by those tall rock formations near the river where the other prisoners you have executed are buried."

"All right," Chinando said.

The door closed, and the law officers were gone.

In their cell, Python and Cobra sat down together on one of the bunks and began to talk in a whisper about ways they might make their escape.

When Roxudi arrived at the police station early the next morning, he found Captain Chinando talking with two middle-aged Cherokee chiefs wearing their full headdresses. Chinando introduced Roxudi to the chiefs, then explained that they were from the Alabama Cherokee area in Indian Territory and had come to ask him for help in settling a dispute between two groups of Cherokees.

"I have had to handle situations like this on a few occasions since I have been captain here, Roxudi," Chinando said. "It seems that the offenders will not listen to any of my officers, but will listen to me because of my rank. So it is best that I go and try to settle this."

"I understand, Captain," Roxudi said. "I will do my best to keep things in order here."

"I appreciate that. I will tell the prisoners why I have to be gone for a while and not to give you any trouble. I will warn them that if they do, they will suffer the consequences."

Roxudi stayed with the two chiefs, learning details about the dispute among their people while Captain Chinando was in the jail, laying out his decree to the prisoners.

Moments later, the captain returned and told Roxudi that he was to check on the prisoners from time to time, and if any of them spoke abusively to him, he was to report it to him when he returned.

In the jail, Python and Cobra were at their cell window, which gave them a view of the hitch rails in front of the station, and watched as Captain Chinando and the chiefs rode away.

"All right," Python said to his brother, "time to put our plan in motion."

Roxudi was sweeping dirt and sand that had been tracked into the building into a dustpan when he heard loud moans coming from the jail building. These were followed by a loud shout, "Hey, Roxudi! Roxudi, come quick! My brother is very sick! Hurry!"

Roxudi laid down the broom and dustpan and ran to the jail building. All the prisoners had their attention fixed on the cell where Cobra lay on his back on the floor, his entire body shaking. He was rolling his head from side to side, and saliva dribbled from his mouth as he moaned loudly. Python was kneeling beside him, holding him by the arms, apparently trying to keep his brother from hurting himself.

"My brother is having one of his seizures! You've got to help him!"

"What can I do?" Roxudi asked. "He needs a doctor, and the closest one is at Fort Gibson. I cannot leave the office to take him. Captain Chinando is gone."

"*You* can help him!" Python said. "When this happens to him, he must be completely submerged in cool water. I know there's a water tank around here for the horses. You must hurry and put Cobra in the tank. If you don't, he will die, and his death will be your fault! The captain will be angry if he doesn't get to hang Cobra when he hangs me, and it will be *your* fault!"

Roxudi chewed his lower lip while the other prisoners looked on.

"Well?" said Python as his brother continued to writhe on the floor.

Roxudi's key ring was on his belt, and a pair of handcuffs lay on a small table by the outside door. "All right," he said, stepping to the table and picking up the handcuffs, "I will have to cuff him first. You move over there by the window and put your back to the wall."

When Python did as he was told, Roxudi moved up to the cell door and inserted the key into the lock.

It was coming up on noon when officers Dan Atkins and Britt Claiborne were on their regular patrol along a riverbank.

"Where do you want to stop and eat lunch today, Britt?" Dan asked.

"Anywhere along here would be fine. You pick the place."

Suddenly, Dan and Britt were stunned to see Python and Cobra rise up from behind some bushes on the riverbank twenty yards ahead of them, rifles in hand.

There was a savage diapason of yells as the killers opened fire.

Dan was hit instantly and buckled in the saddle while Britt whipped out his revolver. He saw the muzzle of one Indian's rifle blossom red and felt the lashing heat of the slug against his cheek as his own gun bucked in his fist.

It was early afternoon when Walugo rode toward the Claiborne cabin and noticed that his daughter was hanging up her wash on the clothesline in back.

Cherokee Rose saw her father get off his horse and walk toward her, and she paused in hanging a pillowcase on the line. "Hello, Father. Did you have a nice visit with Pastor Ward and Sylvia?"

"I did, honey, but while I was at their cabin, some young men came by and told us that there was an escape this morning at the jail attached to the station Britt works out of."

Her eyes widened. "Really?"

"Yes. The young Cherokees told us that they had just talked with Washdino. You know him—he and his wife talked to us after your mother died, trying to console us."

"Yes, I know Washdino."

"Well, Washdino told the young men that he had gone by the station this morning to see Captain Chinando. He did not find him in the office, so he went into the jail building looking for him. The men in the cells told him that Captain Chinando had gone with two Alabama Cherokee men to handle a problem among some of their people and had left his new assistant, Roxudi, to look after things.

"Then they called Washdino's attention to Roxudi's dead body lying in a cell. They told him that Python and Cobra had tricked Roxudi into unlocking their cell, and both of them jumped him. They strangled him and left on foot."

Cherokee Rose's features had gone pale. "Oh, I am so sorry to hear about Roxudi being killed. I am sure when Captain Chinando returns, he will gather some of his men and go after those vicious killers."

"I am sure he will." Walugo sighed. "Well, I must be going. I figured you would want to know about Python and Cobra's escape."

"Yes, thank you for letting me know."

When her father rode away, Cherokee Rose finished hanging

up the wash, then entered the cabin, still thinking about Python and Cobra. A chill ran down her spine. *What if they decide to seek revenge on Britt and Dan for arresting them?*

She pondered it for a few minutes, then told herself that the two escapees would certainly want to get into Seminole territory as fast as they could to elude capture by Captain Chinando.

She kept busy with her daily tasks, but as the hours passed, her mind was soon running wild with concern. She stopped in the middle of kneading bread, went to her knees at a kitchen chair, and asked the Lord to keep her beloved husband safe and to help her to trust Him and to take away her fear.

Cherokee Rose stood to her feet and dried the tears from her cheeks with the bottom of her apron. She went back to kneading the bread and readying the yeasty loaves for the oven. A measure of peace filled her heart, and she hummed a favorite hymn.

fourteen

hen the sun was setting over Indian Territory, Cherokee Rose stood at the front window of the cabin, looking for her husband. She expected him to come riding in on Blackie any minute. After waiting for some time, she returned to the kitchen and moved the steaming pans and the skillet to the cooler side of the stove.

"Britt should have been home almost an hour ago," she said in a low voice. "What can be keeping him?"

She headed back toward the parlor, and when she stepped up to the window and looked outside, a frown creased her brow. There was still no sign of Britt.

There was a scratching at the back of her mind. Maybe Python and Cobra really did go after Britt and Dan.

A trembling hand went to her cheek. "No! No, it cannot be that. It has to be something else. Lord, I want Britt to come home unharmed and tell me about whatever unexpected thing it was that made him late."

She began pacing around the parlor, and all the while a litany was ascending to heaven. "Please, Lord, keep my dear one safe."

She stopped at a small table by the sofa, where her Bible lay. She picked it up and turned to Psalm 66 and read verses 19 and 20 out loud: "'But verily God hath heard me; he hath attended to the voice of my prayer. Blessed be God, which hath not turned away my prayer, nor his mercy from me.' Lord, You know I have claimed these verses before when I have come to You in prayer over something that was heavy on my heart. Father in heaven, please bring my Britt home safely to me."

Cherokee Rose closed her Bible, laid it on the table, and hurried back to the kitchen to check on the food that was on the stove. When she saw that it was staying warm, she hurried back to the parlor and approached the window once again. The twilight on the rolling plains accentuated the forlorn feeling that was overtaking her.

Suddenly, she saw a black horse in the distance, trotting toward the cabin. She smiled, but the smile quickly vanished. The horse was definitely Blackie. But he carried no rider.

Cherokee Rose's heart was thudding in her chest as she ran to the door and out onto the porch. She stepped to the ground just as Blackie drew up and whinnied at her.

She saw blood on the saddle, and she gasped as she stepped up close. The saddle was covered with blood. Her breath caught in her throat. "Oh, no! Oh, no! What has happened?"

Cherokee Rose laid a hand on the side of the gelding's head, her body trembling. "Oh, Blackie, I wish you could talk to me!"

She tied Blackie's reins to one of the posts that supported the porch roof and ran down the path toward her father's cabin, no more than a hundred yards away. She drew up to Walugo's cabin and saw lantern light glowing in a rear window. She pushed the front door open and called out, "Father! Father!"

She could hear rapid footsteps, and when her father appeared, there was enough light for him to see her fear-filled eyes. Walugo grasped her by the shoulders. "What is it, daughter? What is wrong?"

"Father, it—it—"

"What? What?"

Cherokee Rose put a trembling hand to her mouth, closed her eyes, and took a deep breath. She tried to form the words, but nothing coherent came out.

Walugo squeezed her shoulders. "Please calm down, girl. I cannot understand what you are trying to tell me."

She took another deep breath and said in a quavering whisper, "Blackie…just came home with…without Britt. And there is…there is blood on the saddle."

"Oh, no!"

Cherokee Rose's voice grew stronger. "Father, I have been fighting a horrible fear ever since you told me about the jailbreak. It came to me that Python and Cobra just might seek revenge against Britt and Dan for putting them in jail. I am afraid…I am afraid that is what has happened."

"I will saddle up my horse and ride to the police station," Walugo said. "Since there is a full moon tonight, I will be able to look the area over as I ride. You should go tell Pastor Ward about Blackie having returned without Britt. And also your grandparents and Aunt Tarbee."

She nodded.

Walugo put his arms around his daughter. "I understand your fear for Britt, sweet girl, and I am having a hard time myself. But you and I must remember that God has His mighty hand on His born-again children. We must trust Him in this."

"I know, Father, but…but I cannot help being frightened."

"I understand. A Scripture verse just came to mind that I have leaned on many times. Deuteronomy 31:8: 'And the LORD, he it is that doth go before thee; he will be with thee, he will not fail thee, neither forsake thee: fear not, neither be dismayed.'"

Walugo loosened his arms from around his daughter and looked into her eyes, which were now filled with tears. "The Lord is always faithful to His own. At times we do not understand His ways, but they are always right…like when He took your mother home to be with Him. But I could never wish her back into this sinful world now that she is in His presence. We must trust that whatever we find concerning Britt is God's will and that He always does right. Do not give up. Britt may still be alive."

She nodded and sniffed. "I will trust my heavenly Father in this."

"Good girl. Remember the little one you carry, and take extra care."

Walugo headed toward the small corral at the rear of the cabin by the pale light of the rising moon.

Cherokee Rose placed both of her hands on the small mound below her heart. "We must be brave and strong for your father, sweet baby. We must trust our Lord and not be afraid."

Walugo put his horse to a gallop as he headed toward the police station. By the time he arrived there, he had not seen anything along the way to indicate what had happened to Britt. As he pulled rein, three men carrying kerosene lanterns came out of the station building, and he recognized Captain Chinando and two of his officers, Lortho and Emani.

"Hello, Walugo," the captain said. "Do you know about the jailbreak?"

"Yes, sir," said Walugo, dismounting. "I was told about it right about noon."

"Well, I just got back a few minutes ago, and I am very concerned that Officers Atkins and Claiborne have not yet reported in. We are going to see if we can find them."

"There is something you should know, Captain," Walugo said. Then he quickly told Chinando about Britt's horse returning to the Claiborne cabin alone with a great deal of blood on the saddle.

"All the more reason to find Dan and Britt as fast as we can," the captain said.

"Could I go along?"

"Of course, Walugo."

The four mounted up and rode at a gallop by the light of the moon. When they reached the trail that comprised the patrol route of Dan Atkins and Britt Claiborne, they stopped and lit the lanterns, then rode their horses at a trot along the trail.

Soon they reached the river that ran alongside the trail, and within less than ten minutes, Lortho pulled rein and said, "Captain! Over there by the river! There's a body lying on the bank!"

The other three stopped their horses, and Chinando guided his horse toward the spot where the body was lying, with Walugo and the two officers behind him. As they drew up, they could see that the dead man was facedown with his head, arms, and shoulders submerged in the river.

Lortho and Emani dismounted quickly and hurried to the body as Walugo and Chinando slipped from their saddles.

Lortho and Emani set their lanterns close by on the ground,

pulled the body from the water onto the bank, and turned it over.

"It is Dan Atkins, Captain!" Emani said.

As Walugo and Chinando moved closer, Lortho said, "He has a bullet in his midsection. I would say from the blood on his shirt and trousers that he must have bled to death. Somehow he must have crawled to the river in an attempt to get a drink."

Something caught Chinando's attention near some bushes off to their right a few yards.

Walugo noticed him looking that way. "What is it, Captain?"

Chinando raised his lantern level with his head, staring at what he saw. "There are two more bodies lying over there by those bushes." Even as he spoke, he headed that way.

Walugo followed, and Lortho and Emani picked up their lanterns and hurried after them.

Just as they were drawing up, the captain said, "It's Python and Cobra!"

Emani held his lantern so as to put more light on the corpses. Both had bullets in their chests, and Python had a slug in his forehead. The rifles they had stolen from the police station lay on the ground next to them.

Walugo fixed his eyes on the dead men. *Where is Britt? Where is my son-in-law?*

Captain Chinando looked at the bushes, then at the nearby trail where Dan and Britt had been riding. "It looks to me that these two were hiding in the bushes waiting for the two officers to come along the trail."

The captain saw Walugo doing a panorama of the area within the light of the lanterns. "You're wondering where Britt's body is."

Walugo bit his lower lip. He tried to speak, but his throat tightened up.

Chinando laid a hand on Walugo's shoulder. His voice was soft as he said, "Britt's body must be around here somewhere. We have got to find it."

Walugo sniffed and wiped a palm over his face. "Yes, we must. Maybe Britt made his way to the riverbank, too. I have to think that he was on his horse for several minutes after he was shot in order to bleed so much on his saddle."

"I was thinking the same thing," Chinando said. "We need to search the bank for his body."

The four of them walked the bank of the river by lantern light for half an hour and found no sign of Britt's body.

"Britt may well have fallen into the river and floated downstream," Chinando said. "If so, the body may never be found." He noted the look of despair on Walugo's face. "But Lortho, Emani, and I will ride the bank downstream tomorrow and see what we can find."

Walugo nodded. "All right, Captain. I am grateful you are willing to do that. Well, I must go tell my daughter that we found Dan's body but not Britt's. Let us know how it goes tomorrow."

"I certainly will."

Walugo's stomach was in knots as he rode toward the Claiborne cabin. How was Cherokee Rose going to take it when he told her what they had found...and what they had not found?

At the Claiborne cabin, Cherokee Rose had put Blackie in the small corral with White Star and was washing the blood off Britt's saddle in the kitchen when she heard a knock on the front door. Laying the wet cloth down, she dried her hands on a towel and rushed to the front door. Two lanterns burning in the parlor showed her the haggard face of her father when she opened the door.

"Come in, Father," she said. "Do you have bad news?"

Walugo closed the door behind him and took his daughter into his arms. While holding her, he told her in a strained voice what he and the law officers had found on the riverbank beside Britt and Dan's patrol trail.

She leaned back in her father's arms, looked him in the eye, and said with a trembling voice, "Oh, Father, since you did not find Britt's body, he just has to still be alive."

Walugo caressed her cheek. "Honey, with all that blood on his saddle, I…well, it does not look good."

She pressed her face against his chest and sobbed. "Why did the Lord allow this to happen? We have a baby coming!"

Walugo did his best to comfort her as she continued to sob.

After several minutes, Cherokee Rose looked at him through her tears and said, "You are right, Father. Britt had to have been seriously wounded to lose all that blood. He must…he must have died, being wounded like that."

Walugo told her that Captain Chinando and two of his officers were going to ride the riverbank the next day and search for Britt's body. "Honey, if the Lord has taken Britt home to heaven, as He did Dan, He will give you and me and the rest of the family the grace to accept it."

Cherokee Rose took a deep breath and said, "Father, I would like to have my grandparents and my aunt here with me. And Pastor Ward and Sylvia also."

Walugo caressed her cheek again. "I will go tell them what has happened and ask them to come back here with me."

As her father dashed away into the night, Cherokee Rose dropped to her knees at a chair in the parlor and wept as she asked the Lord to give her strength and grace in the midst of her grief.

In just over twenty minutes, Walugo returned with Bando, Nevarra, Tarbee, and the Wards at his side. They all gathered around the grieving expectant mother, attempting to comfort her.

Pastor Ward had them all sit down in the parlor. With his Bible in hand, he pulled a wooden chair in front of the sofa where Cherokee Rose sat between her aunt and her grandmother.

After the pastor read several passages to her from God's Word, Cherokee Rose wiped tears and said, "I know the Lord must have had a reason to take Britt to heaven and leave me here to raise our baby without a father."

Pastor Ward nodded and said, "You and I know that our heavenly Father does not make mistakes. Even if we do not always understand His ways, whatever He does is always right and good."

"This makes me think of Job, Pastor. When his seven sons and three daughters were all killed at one time, it grieved him beyond description. Even though his heart was broken, he said, 'The LORD gave, and the LORD hath taken away; blessed be the name of the LORD.'"

Tears were flowing once again down Cherokee Rose's cheeks. "Oh, Pastor Ward, though I do not know how I will make it without Britt, I want God to be able to say of me as He said of Job, 'In all this Job sinned not, nor charged God foolishly.'"

Everyone in the group had tears in their eyes as they saw just what kind of Christian Cherokee Rose was.

Nevarra took hold of Cherokee Rose's hand. "We have suffered many sorrows this past year, but the Lord has been close to those of us who belong to Him. And now, with Britt being taken from us, the Lord will help us weather this storm together. You and your baby will always be loved and cared for by your family and by your people. It is hard to understand this tragedy, but we know from God's Word that His grace is sufficient. For peace and strength in our sorrow, we must cling to this wonderful truth."

Cherokee Rose looked into her grandmother's kind eyes. "You are right, Grandmother. And though the days ahead will be hard, we have each other, and we know that our Saviour is the same yesterday and today and forever."

Everyone in the room was wiping tears and nodding.

Cherokee Rose ran her gaze over their faces, and a small, thin smile curved her lips. She laid a hand on her midsection. "I have this little one who is nestled close to my heart to care for, and I must honor my husband by seeing that this baby is loved and given a good home. I intend to do just that."

Pastor Ward looked at her with admiration, then ran his eyes across the faces of the others. "Let's pray."

As the pastor prayed, he asked the Lord to give Cherokee Rose His comfort and His sufficient grace in her time of sorrow.

fifteen

arly the next morning, Pastor Layne Ward and his wife, Sylvia, were just finishing breakfast when they heard the sound of hoofbeats at the front of the cabin, the snort of a horse, and male voices.

"I'll see who it is, sweetheart," Layne said, skidding his chair back from the table.

When the pastor opened the front door, Captain Chinando was on the porch and Officers Lortho and Emani were on their horses. A body was draped over Lortho's horse behind the saddle.

"Walugo told me that Officer Dan Atkins was a member of your church, Pastor," Chinando said.

Ward nodded. "Yes."

"We have brought the body to you so you could see that it is buried. We figured you would want to have a burial service."

"I appreciate you doing this, Chinando. Please have your officers take the body behind the cabin and place it on the back porch. I will conduct the funeral service for Officer Atkins at one o'clock tomorrow afternoon and also have a memorial service for Officer Claiborne after Officer Atkins's body is buried."

Chinando nodded, then turned and said to his companions, "Pastor Ward wants us to place Officer Atkins's body on the back porch of the cabin."

While the officers carried the lifeless form toward the rear of the cabin, Layne said to Chinando, "Walugo told Mrs. Ward and me last night that you're going to make a thorough search for Officer Claiborne's body today."

"Yes, we are going to ride the banks of the river. Since we could not find a trace of the body last night where the shoot-out took place, I suspect that Officer Claiborne may have fallen in the river after he was shot. All we can do is try to find it, though we know it may never be found."

"Please let me know how the search goes, will you?"

"I certainly will, Pastor Ward."

For the entire day, Captain Chinando and his two officers rode the banks of the river downstream from where the shoot-out between Dan Atkins and Britt Claiborne and the two Seminole Indians had taken place.

Twilight was on the land when Captain Chinando knocked

on the door of the Ward cabin that evening. When the pastor opened the door, Captain Chinando said, "Good evening, Pastor Ward. We have just returned from our search. We found no trace of Officer Claiborne's body."

The heaviness of heart that the pastor felt showed on his features as he said, "Thank you for taking the time to come and let me know. I guess we'll never know for sure what happened to Britt. I'll go and tell Walugo."

At one o'clock on Friday afternoon, October 4, a large crowd gathered at the burial ground where Dan Atkins's body, wrapped in a blanket, lay on a stretcher next to an open grave. In the crowd were several Indian Territory policemen, including Chief Yasson and Captain Chinando.

Cherokee Rose, flanked by Sylvia Ward on one side and her grandmother, Nevarra, on the other, huddled near the body and the grave. Walugo, Chief Bando, and Tarbee stood next to Nevarra.

Chief Sequoyah and Chief John Ross stood close by Pastor Layne Ward at the head of the stretcher to conduct the funeral service.

Pastor Ward told the audience briefly about the shoot-out between Dan Atkins and Britt Claiborne and the escaped killers, Python and Cobra. He told of the search for Officer Claiborne's body, and of Captain Chinando's conclusion that the body must have floated down the river and finally sunk into its depths. He informed the crowd that after the service for Dan, he would have a memorial service for Britt.

Cherokee Rose wept as the pastor told the story. Sylvia Ward and Nevarra each had an arm around her, squeezing her tightly.

At one point, Cherokee Rose placed both trembling hands on

the small mound beneath her heart. While the tears ran down her ashen cheeks and dripped off her chin, she spoke to her unborn child. *My precious little one, your father would have loved you so much. I will always do my best to keep him alive in your mind when you are old enough to understand. With God's help, you and I will do our best to honor him even though he is not with us.*

Her attention was then drawn to Pastor Ward, who was telling the crowd about Britt leading Dan to Christ and about Dan being baptized the following Sunday as a testimony to his salvation.

The pastor then opened his Bible and read several Scriptures about salvation and about heaven, stating that because Dan had received the Lord Jesus as his Saviour, he was now in heaven with Him.

When Pastor Ward finished his message, he implored those who had never been saved to come to him later, and he would help them to come to Christ.

Four police officers then solemnly lowered Dan's body into the grave.

With this done, the pastor began his memorial service for Britt Claiborne. First, he spoke comforting words to Cherokee Rose; then he told the crowd what a solid Christian Britt had been, in addition to the fact that he had been an excellent army officer and a top-notch policeman.

Pastor Ward then looked at the teary-eyed Cherokee Rose and said, "I am asking all of you who are Christians to hold Officer Claiborne's widow up in prayer." He paused while wiping tears from his own face. "Mrs. Claiborne is expecting her first child. Please pray for the baby, too, who will be born into this world without a father."

Pastor Ward noticed a wagon pull into the burial ground close by and head toward the grave site. Three men sat on the driver's seat. Suddenly Ward's heart lurched, then thudded in his chest, and he could no longer speak.

Everyone in the crowd could hear the rattle of the wagon as it drew up. When they saw the wagon's effect on the pastor, they all turned and looked that way.

Cherokee Rose was aware that the pastor had gone silent, but she didn't notice the wagon. She was looking at the ground beneath her feet, her mind fixed on the fact that she was a young widow left to raise her child alone.

Slowly she became aware of a babble of voices and looked up to see the people turned so they could look behind them. She followed their line of sight and saw a man in a police uniform alight from the wagon. She thought her mind was hallucinating. She wiped the tears from her eyes, then looked at him again. He was coming toward her. A sharp gasp escaped her lips, and she put her hands to her mouth.

"Grandmother!" she said. "It is Britt! He is alive!"

Cherokee Rose broke free from the loose hold Nevarra and Sylvia had on her and ran toward the man who was hurrying toward her. Britt gathered her into his arms and held her tight.

"Oh, Britt," she said with a quavering voice, "I thought my mind was playing tricks on me. We all thought you were dead!"

"It's really me, sweetheart, alive and well," Britt said as he kissed her cheek. "I'm sorry I worried you and the family. It's a long story, but I'm fine, and I'm here with you!"

She embraced him with a strong hold. "Oh, thank You, Lord!" she cried. "Thank You! You *did* hear me. You *did* attend to the voice of my prayer. Blessed be God, who hath not turned away my prayer, nor withheld His mercy from me!"

Everyone looked on, smiling, and the Christians were praising the Lord for sparing Britt's life.

Cherokee Rose looked into Britt's eyes and told him about Blackie coming home alone with blood on the saddle and of Captain Chinando and the two officers searching for his body.

Britt nodded. "My two Cherokee friends here, Chief Vandigo and Armido, were taking me in their wagon to our cabin. One of the older men in the area saw us and told me that Pastor Ward was holding the funeral service for Dan here at the burial ground."

"Yes, and a memorial service for *you*," spoke up Pastor Ward, smiling at Britt.

"You do not seem to be wounded," Cherokee Rose said, looking her husband up and down.

"No, thank the Lord, I'm not."

Her brow furrowed. "But there was a lot of blood on your saddle."

Britt noted the curious looks on everyone's faces and said, "Let me explain. Many of you know that Dan Atkins and I were partners on the job and had become close friends. Dan often spoke of how much he liked my horse, Blackie, and he asked me on Tuesday if I would switch with him sometime and let him ride Blackie while I rode his horse. I told him we could do it the next day. So…on Wednesday morning, before we started on our patrol, we switched horses."

Britt went on to tell the crowd how Python and Cobra had waited in ambush by the river, knowing that he and Dan would be riding through that area.

Britt held Cherokee Rose's hand as he went on to say that when Python and Cobra rose up from behind some bushes and opened fire, a bullet hit Dan, and he buckled over in the saddle aboard Blackie. Britt whipped out his revolver and began firing back just as a bullet meant for him barely missed hitting him in the head. At that point, he hopped off of Dan's horse, took refuge behind a large rock, and kept firing.

The crowd listened intently as Britt pointed to Armido and said, "Armido's brother, Pidini, was riding his horse that day along the riverbank, alone. He drew rein at the sound of the gunfire, then saw me crouched low behind the rock, firing at the two Seminoles. Pidini recognized me and realized I was in a shoot-out with apparent outlaws and decided to join me. In the midst of the shoot-out, Pidini moved toward another rock to have a better vantage point. When he did, he was hit with a bullet in his upper thigh.

"Though he dropped to one knee, he kept firing, and between the two of us, we were able to cut down those two killers. By this time, Dan had fallen from Blackie's back and had crawled to the edge of the river, but he was dead.

"Knowing there was nothing I could do for Dan, I saw that Pidini's thigh wound was bleeding heavily. I told him I would make a tourniquet and take him to the doctor at Fort Gibson. But Pidini told me that his home at Pine Mountain was much closer, and there was a retired doctor there who could take care of his wound.

"I was glad for the shorter distance to get the help Pidini needed, but I knew he could not stay on his horse unless I rode with him. I ripped off one of Pidini's shirt sleeves and used it as a tourniquet on his thigh. I told myself I would return later to the river to pick up Dan's body and take Blackie home.

"As Pidini and I rode toward Pine Mountain, his gelding stepped in a hole. We hit the ground rolling. As soon as I found that Pidini was all right, I saw that the gelding had broken his leg, so I had to carry Pidini the rest of the way. It took two days.

"Well, that's the story. I'm glad to report that Pidini is doing fine." Britt took a deep breath and looked down at his wife. "That's why I just now made it back home."

Cherokee Rose nodded and gave him a smile.

Pastor Ward moved up close to Britt and Cherokee Rose and said to the crowd, "I know we are all very thankful that Officer Claiborne is still with us. Let's sing a hymn of praise to the Lord for protecting him in the shoot-out."

Layne led them in a hymn as many people in the crowd shed tears.

That evening, when Britt and Cherokee Rose were alone in their cabin, she told Britt about the passage in the book of Job that she had claimed as her own when she thought he had been killed. With tears of joy flowing once more, she said, "Darling, I am glad the Lord can say of your wife, 'In all this Cherokee Rose sinned not, nor charged God foolishly.'"

Britt took her in his arms and kissed her tenderly. "I am sure the Lord is pleased with how you handled the blow of thinking you had become a widow and would have to raise our child by yourself." He kissed her again, then said, "I love you more than ever."

"And this baby and I both love *you* more than ever."

Britt folded her in his arms once more and held her close. She laid her head on his chest.

"Our wonderful Lord is the God of miracles," she said, then eased back and looked into his eyes. "I never want to doubt His love and His mercy."

"I don't either, sweetheart."

More tears filled her eyes, and she laid her head on his chest again. He squeezed her tight, and she could hear the steady beat of his heart. *Thank You, precious Lord, that his heart is still beating.*

Cherokee Rose thumbed the tears from her eyes and said, "Officer Claiborne…"

"Yes, ma'am?"

"Please do not ever scare me this way again."

He laughed and kissed her forehead. "I'll do my best to comply with that request, my dear. Let's thank the Lord together for His merciful grace to us in this whole thing."

While Britt held his wife close to his heart, the two of them humbled themselves before their loving heavenly Father, pouring out their praise to Him.

n Monday morning, October 7, the sun rose in a golden blaze as Cherokee General Council chairman Thundro stood outside the brick building that housed the offices and meeting hall. Twenty young Cherokee men stood before him, holding the reins of their horses. They were messengers who often carried information from the Council to the chiefs all over the portion of Indian Territory occupied by the Cherokees.

The sun reflected off the twin towers above the front door, and at the same time, the rolling hills and shallowed valleys on the surrounding prairie took on wondrous changing hues.

The chairman stood beside a straight-backed wooden chair, which had a stack of papers on the seat.

"Men, today you will be carrying a printed notice to all the Cherokee chiefs in the Territory," Thundro said. "As you will see, the notice announces that a very important meeting has been scheduled here at the Cherokee General Council headquarters to formally establish the United Cherokee Nation. The notice urges all chiefs to attend."

A flock of blackbirds appeared overhead, making their usual screeching. The messengers glanced up at them as did the chairman.

When the sound of the noisy birds began to lessen, Thundro said, "You men have all been given your assigned areas where you are to deliver the notices." He paused, looked at one of the messengers, and said, "Megalon, you will be taking over the area usually covered by Kulondo, since he is still not feeling well. It includes the section under Chief Bando. Come and talk to me before you ride."

With that, Thundro dismissed the messengers, telling them to come and pick up the printed notices.

Megalon approached the chairman and said, "What did you want to talk to me about, sir?"

"Chief John Ross lives in the section under Chief Bando. Make sure that he gets one of these notices, and I also want you to tell him that I said it is very important that he be here."

"I will do that," Megalon said.

Later that morning, Chief John Ross and Chief Bando stood in front of Bando's cabin, talking about the great-grandchild that Cherokee Rose was going to bring into the world for Nevarra and Bando to love and enjoy.

Ross smiled and said, "I can only try to imagine what it is like to be a parent, my friend. Even to be a grandparent. But when I try to imagine myself as a *great-grandparent*, my mind goes into a whirl!"

Bando noticed a rider coming along the path, running his gaze at the surrounding cabins. When the rider fixed his attention on Bando's cabin, he made his horse move faster.

On his horse, Megalon looked at the dark-skinned man as he drew up and said, "Are you Chief Bando? A Cherokee boy just gave me directions to this cabin."

"I am," said Bando, smiling. "What can I do for you?"

"Chief Bando, my name is Megalon. I am a messenger for Chairman Thundro of the Cherokee General Council in Tahlequah." He slipped a folded paper from his shirt pocket and extended it to Bando. "I have this notice for you. It concerns a very important meeting scheduled at ten o'clock on Tuesday morning, October 15, at the Council headquarters building. At that meeting, the United Cherokee Nation will be formally established. All Cherokee chiefs are getting the notice today, and as you will see, every chief is urged to be there."

Bando accepted the paper and unfolded it.

While he was looking at it, Megalon said, "Chief Bando, can you tell me where I might find Chief John Ross? I understand he lives in this section."

Bando smiled and pointed to the lighter-skinned man. "This is Chief John Ross."

"I am glad to meet you, Chief John Ross." Megalon took another printed notice from his shirt pocket and handed it to Ross. "I have a special message to you from Chairman Thundro."

"Yes?"

"He asked me to tell you that it is very important that you be present at the meeting."

Ross nodded. "You can tell him that I will be there."

"Megalon, I am quite sure all the North Carolina Cherokee chiefs will be there," Chief Bando said.

Megalon smiled. "That will be very good, Chief Bando. I hope all the other Cherokee chiefs will be there, too. Well, I must be going. I have more stops to make."

Bando turned to Ross as Megalon rode away. "With Chairman Thundro's insistence that you be at the meeting, my friend, that makes me think the General Council has something special in mind for you."

John shrugged. "Maybe so, but I have no idea what it might be."

It was almost nine o'clock on Tuesday morning, October 15, 1839, when Chief John Ross, Chief Bando, Chief Sequoyah, and several other North Carolina Chiefs drew near Fort Gibson on their way to nearby Tahlequah.

Ross, Bando, and Sequoyah were riding just ahead of the others. Ross turned his head so all could hear him and said, "I am going to stop at the fort to see someone for a few minutes. I will be in Tahlequah in plenty of time before the meeting starts."

The others rode on toward Tahlequah, and John Ross trotted his horse up to the fort's front gate. Both guards recognized and greeted him.

One of them glanced at the other Cherokees, who kept on riding. "Aren't you going to the big meeting, Chief?"

"I am, but I want to see Mary Stapler for a few minutes. The big meeting starts at ten o'clock."

The guards opened the gate for him, and moments later, John pulled rein in front of the medical office. Before he left the saddle, his attention was drawn to the office window. Inside, Mary was using a cloth to wash the window. She saw him and flashed him one of her captivating smiles.

He grinned at her as he left the saddle and headed toward the door. Before he reached it, it came open, and Mary took a couple of backward steps. "Hello, John. Come in."

John closed the door behind him and found Mary looking at him eagerly. Since no one else was in the office or the waiting area, he opened his arms. Mary rushed into them.

After a warm embrace, John held her at arm's length and said, "I wish I could tell you how those marvelous smiles you always give me affect my heart."

She flashed him another one. "Really? Well, give it a try."

"All right. Each time you smile at me like that, it affects my heart like…like the warm sun affects snow."

"No one has ever said that about my smiles before."

He kissed her cheek, then looked with admiration into her eyes. "You are such a special lady."

"Oh, John, you shouldn't put me on a pedestal."

They shared a brief but tender kiss, then John said, "I must head for the big meeting at the Cherokee General Council headquarters."

"I was about to ask you if that's why you're here."

"Yes. I have no idea how long it will last, but even if it runs late, I will come by your father's house and see you again before I head for home."

She nodded. "Well, if you get here before suppertime, you are invited to eat with us."

"I'll take you up on that!" John took hold of her shoulders and kissed her again. Then gently cupping her face in his hands, he said, "I love you, Mary."

With that, he hurried to the door. When he opened it, he looked back at her. The silence made his heart begin to flutter with something like fear. Then she smiled at him and said, "I love you, too!"

He sighed and said, "I was hoping to hear those words!"

Then he hurried to his horse, mounted up, and rode away.

Mary stood at the open door and watched John ride out of sight, then moved inside and closed the door. As she walked to the window and picked up the wet cloth she had dropped, she said, "I thought when my husband was killed that I would always remain a lonely widow. Thank You, Lord, that You had different plans for me. As this relationship between John and me develops, please help me to be ever faithful to Your perfect will for my life."

At exactly ten o'clock that morning, Thundro stepped to the front of the large platform in the spacious meeting hall and ran his gaze over the crowd of Cherokee chiefs.

Seated on the platform behind Thundro were the fifty-six men who made up the Council. Thundro was pleased that all the Cherokee chiefs of Indian Territory were in attendance.

"I want to welcome all of you," Chairman Thundro said with a broad smile. "I very much appreciate your attendance here today to join the Council and me in officially establishing the United Cherokee Nation."

The crowd applauded.

Thundro then laid out the plans for them, explaining how the new United Cherokee Nation would function. When he was done, he asked for questions from the floor.

A few chiefs had some questions, and between Thundro and the men of the Council, all the questions were satisfactorily answered.

The chiefs then listened intently as Thundro read the entire constitution to them. When he was finished, there were contented smiles on the faces of the Cherokee leaders.

"Are there any questions about the constitution?" Thundro said.

There was dead silence.

A pleasant look framed his rugged features. "Well, if there are no questions, we will proceed to take the vote to—"

"Chairman Thundro," cut in a silver-haired chief as he rose from his seat. "I do not have a question, but I have something I would like to say about the constitution."

"All right, Chief Rismando. Let us hear it."

"I would just like to say that I like the constitution very much. Chief John Ross did a magnificent job putting it together. It will make our new United Cherokee Nation strong."

The other chiefs raised their voices in affirmation.

"Before I present the vote to establish the new Nation and accept the constitution as it stands," Thundro said, "I want to ask Chief John Ross to come to the platform."

Ross, who was seated a few rows from the platform between Chief Bando and Chief Sequoyah, rose to his feet. There were some pleasant murmurings among the crowd as Ross walked to the platform, climbed the steps, and shook the chairman's hand.

Thundro then led Ross to the raised speaker's desk and said, "Chief John Ross, before these great Cherokee leaders, I want to commend you for your magnificent accomplishment in producing the constitution for our new government."

Suddenly, the chiefs began to stand up all over the meeting hall, applauding and shouting out their appreciation. The ovation lasted for nearly a minute. Then as the chiefs went quiet and sat down, Chairman Thundro asked Ross to stay at his side.

"We will now take the vote," Thundro said. "Will everyone who wishes to adopt this constitution for our new nation, please stand."

Everyone stood, and they all applauded and cheered when Thundro pronounced the United Cherokee Nation now in existence.

When the applauding and cheering subsided, Thundro said, "Now, I wish to bring up a very important matter. My friends, our next item of business is this: We need to elect a president of our new Nation."

Thundro glanced over his shoulder at the councilmen behind him, then looked back at the chiefs. "I have already made a strong recommendation to the Council that a certain Cherokee man who has established himself as a great leader among our people should be the president of our new nation." Thundro smiled at the crowd. "All of you know of whom I speak."

There was sudden cheering, with many voices calling out the name of Chief John Ross. While the cheering went on, Ross looked at the chairman, who only smiled at him.

When there was silence once more, Thundro set his gaze on Ross. "Chief John Ross, would you accept the presidency of the new United Cherokee Nation? And I must add that if you do accept this position, you would need to establish your residence in Tahlequah, because it will be the capital, and the president's office will be here in this building."

Ross licked his lips and looked down at Chief Bando. The chief gave him a nod and a smile, and Ross said so all could hear, "Chairman Thundro, if the Council and the chiefs elect me as president, I will be honored beyond words, and I will be glad to establish my home in Tahlequah."

There was more applause and cheering all over the meeting

hall, and when it died down, Chairman Thundro recommended that Chief John Ross be elected president of the new United Cherokee Nation.

The vote was unanimous.

Thundro then announced that Thursday, October 24, would be Inauguration Day in Tahlequah. The chiefs would give word to all the Cherokee people in Indian Territory that Chief John Ross had been elected president and would take his oath of office on that day. All Cherokees in the Nation would be urged to attend.

seventeen

ohn Ross rode toward Fort Gibson, his heart pounding in his chest. He was eager to tell Mary Stapler that he had been elected president of the new United Cherokee Nation and would be moving to Tahlequah very soon.

It was just past four thirty in the afternoon when the guards at the fort opened the front gate to let Ross ride in. When he drew up in front of Dr. Robert Miles's office and dismounted, John was going over in his mind the plan he had devised for breaking the news to Mary. He would tell her that the new United Cherokee Nation had been established at the meeting and was now in force. He would then say that the Council and the chiefs had also voted in a president to lead the Nation. When Mary asked who the president was, he would give her a sly grin and say, "You are looking at him."

John chuckled to himself as he tied the reins to the hitch rail, thinking of the fun he would have breaking the news to Mary in this manner. He had taken two steps toward the office when he was surprised to see Mary come out the door with a wide smile on her face.

"Good afternoon, Mr. President!" she said.

John's brow furrowed. He was about to ask Mary how she knew about his election when her father came out the door and said, "Congratulations, John! Wow! My daughter and I are so honored that a man of your stature would humble himself to step on our property."

John chuckled nervously. "How did you two find out?"

"A couple of Alabama Cherokee chiefs came in a while ago," Mary said. "One of them needed some salve for a skin rash he has, and while they were here, they told us about Chief John Ross being elected president of the new nation. They said that your inauguration will take place in Tahlequah on October 24." Mary moved up to him and embraced him. "Oh, John, I am so proud of you! I know you'll do a wonderful job as president."

Dr. Miles smiled. "My daughter's right. From all I know about you, they picked the best man for the job."

Mary's eyes were twinkling as she said, "Mr. President, will you honor Daddy and me by eating supper with us?"

"I most certainly will!" John said.

❧

The three of them had a good time together during the meal, and when it was time for John to head for home, Dr. Miles told him good night and went to his bedroom.

Mary walked outside with John into the cool evening air, wrapping a shawl around her shoulders. He bragged on her cooking once again as they descended the porch steps. He took her in his arms and set his soft gaze on her by the light of the rising moon. He seemed to study each of her lovely features. He reached out a forefinger and lifted her chin, and they shared a tender kiss.

"Mary, I must tell you that I find more love for you in my heart every day."

She caressed his cheek. "It is the same way with me toward you, John."

As he reluctantly mounted his horse, John told Mary he would be back to Tahlequah within a week or so with his possessions to begin settling into the cabin he had found there that afternoon.

"I will look forward to having you so close, John," she said, giving him another one of her captivating smiles.

"It will be wonderful to be so close to you, sweet Mary. Goodnight. I love you."

"I love you, too," she said. "Goodnight."

As John guided his horse toward the fort's front gate, Mary mounted the porch steps and pulled the shawl up around her neck and shoulders. She watched him until he turned a corner at some barracks, then she sat down in one of the rocking chairs on the porch, memorizing the last few minutes they'd had together before he rode away.

❧

The moon shone brightly over Indian Territory as John Ross trotted his horse over the rolling hills. His mind was fixed on Mary, and his heart seemed to be reaching back for her.

He took a deep breath and said, "Lord, she is the one I want to marry. We both have been alone for some time now, and it would be so good to have a wife and companion by my side. If I am thinking wrong, Lord, I need You to reveal that to me. But if I am thinking correctly, I need to know I am doing Your will by asking her to marry me." John looked up beyond the multitude of twinkling stars above him. "Please, heavenly Father, give me peace in my heart about it if I have Your permission to ask her to marry me."

John sensed a fresh warmth inside him, and a quiet peace flooded his heart. He knew beyond a doubt that it was God's benediction on his plan to ask Mary to become his wife.

A contented sigh escaped his lips as his horse carried him toward what was now his temporary home.

Mary Stapler still sat on the porch, wrapped in her shawl. Suddenly she was startled when she heard her father say, "Mary, I was wondering where you were. I expected to hear you in your room by now."

She looked up at him in the bright moonlight. "Oh, Daddy, the Lord is doing something between John and me. I just know it."

The doctor smiled. "That's the way it looks to me, honey. I sure do like him. He's a fine Christian and a man of wisdom and integrity. But…what are you doing sitting out here in the chilly air?"

Mary stood up. "Oh. Well, I watched John ride away and sort of got caught up in some daydreaming."

Her father chuckled. "I would say you really *are* in love with John."

"Yes, Daddy, I am."

"Has he told you that he loves you?"

"Yes, he has. And, Daddy I really believe John will propose to me soon. If I'm right, what would you think if I accept his proposal?"

The doctor took both of his daughter's hands in his own. "Well, my dear, I know John couldn't find a better bride anywhere, and I know he'll make a fine husband for you. Just think! If this happens, you'll be the wife of the *president*!"

Mary giggled. "Oh, Daddy!"

He squeezed her hands. "Seriously, Mary, I am very glad that John came into your life. Since I believe the Lord is in it, I know the two of you will be very happy together."

Tears misted her eyes. "Will you be able to get along without me in your home?"

"I'll be just fine, honey. I can hire someone to take care of the house and do some cooking for me. An Indian woman possibly. It won't be the same without you, but I want you to be happy. And like I said, I know that you and John will be very happy together. After all you've been through, you more than deserve some happiness." He leaned over and kissed his daughter's cheek. "I think I'll head for bed now. This tired body is telling me it's time."

Mary nodded. "Let's go inside. It is getting pretty chilly out here. And besides, I need to head for dreamland myself."

He opened the door and followed his daughter inside. As they started down the hall, Mary said, "Thank you for backing me in my feelings toward John. Of course, you will always be my very special daddy."

"I know that, honey. And thank you for feeling that way toward me."

"I have every reason to feel that way. You're the best daddy in the whole world."

He smiled and said, "As long as I can keep you thinking that, everything will be okay."

"I don't think it. I *know* it!"

Mary bid her father good night and entered her room. She was pleased to find that her father had lit the lamp on the small table beside her bed.

She removed her dress and donned a soft flannel gown. Taking the pins from her hair, she shook it loose, then stepped to the dresser and picked up a brush. Slowly pulling the brush through her long blond hair, she walked to the window and gazed out at the star-filled sky and the silver moon. "Thank You, Lord, for bringing John into my life. We will indeed be very happy together. I just know it."

Mary slipped into bed, took her Bible from the table that held the lamp, and read a chapter in the Gospel of John. Then she blew out the lamp and pulled the covers up close to her chin. After praying for several minutes, she looked toward the window and whispered, "Good night, President John Ross. Sleep well. I love you."

She pulled the covers up closer to her chin, and soon she was fast asleep with a tiny smile of delight gracing her face.

The next morning, John Ross was just finishing breakfast in his cabin when he heard Chief Bando call his name from outside, near the front porch. When he opened the door, he found a large crowd of Cherokees gathered there with their chief to congratulate him.

At church on Sunday morning, Layne and Sylvia Ward, Britt and Cherokee Rose Claiborne, and Chief Bando and Nevarra sang a gospel song, dedicating it to President John Ross.

On Monday, October 21—six days after he had been elected president of the United Cherokee Nation—John Ross arrived in Tahlequah with two wagons driven by soldiers from Fort Gibson. With the soldiers' help, John's furniture, clothing, kitchen articles, and food were placed in his new cabin.

Once everything was in place, the soldiers drove away, leaving John alone in the spacious cabin. As he slowly walked from room to room, John smiled to himself and said, "I'm sure Mary will want to rearrange a lot of this, but that's okay with me. I know she will be bringing a lot of her own things, and soon this cabin will be a happy home for the two of us." He paused in the parlor and pictured Mary there beside him. "Yes, my sweet Mary, you will indeed make this a warm, cozy home for both of us."

That evening, after John had eaten supper with Mary and her father, he took her to see his cabin. After Mary had been given the tour, they sat down on the overstuffed sofa in the parlor.

"Oh, John, this cabin is better than ever now that you live here and your things are in it."

John looked at her and said, "There is only one thing missing."

"What?"

John slipped off the sofa and went to his knees in front of her. "It is not *what*, darling. It is *who*."

"Who?"

"Yes. *You!*"

"Me?"

"Of course. Mary, will you marry me?"

Her famous smile was brighter than ever when she said, "Yes! Yes, John, I will marry you."

John stood up, and Mary did the same. After they had sealed the engagement with a kiss, they sat down and discussed when they would marry. They agreed that there should be a proper courtship since all eyes in the United Cherokee Nation would be on John as president. They decided to set the date in March.

When they returned to the Miles house, they told Mary's father of the engagement, and he was elated for them.

On Thursday, October 24, thousands of Cherokees from all over Indian Territory and many soldiers from Fort Gibson were in Tahlequah to see President John Ross take his oath of office in front of the Cherokee General Council building. It was a bright, sunny day without a cloud in the sky, though everyone had to dress warm due to the autumn chill.

John Ross stood with Chairman Thundro, and the Cherokee General Council formed a half-circle behind them. Facing the huge crowd, John was pleased to see Mary standing in the first row with her father. When their eyes met, she flashed him her smile, and he felt his heart leap in his chest.

Thundro led the ceremony as John Ross took his oath of office with his hand on a Cherokee Bible. At the close of the oath, there was a great ovation from the crowd. Thundro then called for President Ross's pastor, Layne Ward, to come and pray for the new president, which pleased John greatly.

After Pastor Ward led in prayer, John Ross delivered his acceptance speech. When he finished, he had Mary Stapler stand and explained that they would be married the following March. The crowd cheered its approval.

John then looked at Chief Sequoyah, who stood nearby, and asked him to come stand beside him. There were cheers for the silver-haired chief as he made his way forward. John commended Chief Sequoyah for what he had done to strengthen the Cherokee Nation by giving them an alphabet and by translating the Bible into their language. He then asked him to say a few words.

Chief Sequoyah spoke of how pleased he was that all his Cherokee friends were doing well in their new homeland and said once again that, with all the happiness around him, the stars at night shone with a new brightness.

Tears filled Sequoyah's eyes as the crowd cheered him, and many called out, saying they loved him.

eighteen

By the end of October, all the North Carolina Cherokee church buildings had been completed. As the months passed, each Sunday—unless hindered by bad weather—President John Ross and Mary Stapler traveled southwestward to attend the church pastored by Layne Ward. That building had been completed in late September.

On Sunday afternoon, March 15, 1840, President John Ross and Mary Stapler were wed at their church in North Carolina

Cherokee territory. It was a simple but beautiful ceremony as John and Mary took their vows before God, Pastor Layne Ward, and the crowd inside the packed auditorium. Both of them felt a deep inner peace as they pledged their undying love to one another.

Because it was a warm day, the reception afterward—which included a dinner provided by the women of the church—was held outside. After all the wedding guests passed by to wish the bride and groom well, Mary's father stepped up and shook hands with John, saying how proud he was to have him for his son-in-law. He then embraced Mary, kissed her on the cheek, and explained to both of them that he had to get back to the fort. He had surgery to do on a soldier who had been thrown from a horse that morning and shattered a bone in his right shoulder.

Dr. Miles stepped away from the newlyweds, and Britt and Cherokee Rose Claiborne moved up, smiling.

"Well, President and Mrs. Ross," Britt said, "are you ready to let us sit with you for the meal as you promised?"

"We sure are," replied John, taking hold of his bride's hand.

Mary and Cherokee Rose had spent some time together over the past few months and were becoming good friends. As the Rosses and the Claibornes walked together toward the table reserved for the bride and groom and their special guests, Mary noted that her friend was wincing as she walked, and her gait was awkward.

Mary patted Cherokee Rose's arm and said, "I never had the pleasure of becoming a mother, so I can't tell from experience what it's like to carry a baby, but I can see that you are getting quite uncomfortable."

"That I am, Mary. Most of the time now, I stay pretty close to home. It is becoming more and more difficult to get this ungainly body to function like I want it to." She sighed and smiled. "But I know it will be worth it when I hold that little one in my arms."

They were approaching the reserved table, which was positioned beneath an apple tree that was just beginning to bud. Britt took hold of Cherokee Rose's hand, guided her up to the table, and gently eased her onto a straight-backed wooden chair.

"Sweetheart, is this chair all right, or would you be more comfortable if I got you a pillow to sit on? I've seen some on the pastor's sofa in his office."

Cherokee Rose adjusted herself as best she could and smiled up at her husband. "Don't worry about me. I will be fine. It is just so good to be here with John and Mary."

"Mary will stay here with you while Britt and I go to the food tables and fill your plates," John said.

"Maybe half-full, Britt," Cherokee Rose said. "I am not feeling very hungry today."

"Well, that's a switch," Britt said. "In the last few months, you've been hungry enough to eat for both of us!"

Cherokee Rose and Mary watched their husbands head for the food tables. Cherokee Rose placed both hands on her swollen abdomen, sighed, and said, "Oh, Mary, I love that man so much!"

Mary smiled at her. "That is quite obvious, honey. I hope people will be able to tell that I love John just like you love Britt."

"Oh, don't worry. It already shows."

John and Britt soon returned carrying four plates of food plus four steaming cups of coffee on trays. As the Rosses and the Claibornes sipped their coffee after finishing their meal, people continued to come by to give their best to the president and his new bride.

The visits from well-wishers were lessening when Mary noticed three soldiers coming toward them. She did not recall ever seeing them before, even among the well-wishers who had passed by in the line earlier. As they drew nearer, she noted that all three were privates.

"Looks like we have some more company coming," Mary said to the others in a whisper. "I don't know these soldiers. They must be new at the fort."

When the privates drew up to the table, they had stern looks on their faces. One of them was a big, husky man who dwarfed the other two.

He looked at Mary and said in a deep, gruff voice, "We found out about this weddin' yesterday and that this guy you just married is part Indian. You're all white, ain'tcha?"

John and Britt both stood up at the same instant.

"Yes, my wife is all white, private," John said. "So what?"

"Well, we don't like our kind mixin' with lowdown Indians, that's what! It ain't right!"

John's face reddened, and the sudden anger that whipped up within him tightened his throat so he could not speak. Mary and Cherokee Rose looked at each other, eyes wide.

"It's none of your business who this lady marries, private," Britt said. "Now, all three of you turn around and get out of here before I lose my temper!"

"And just who are you?" the private asked.

Britt stepped around the table and moved up to the big man. "I am Officer Britt Claiborne of the Indian Territory Police."

The big man grinned. "Yeah, sure. How come you ain't in uniform?"

"I don't owe you an explanation. Before you and your pals leave, I want to know your names."

"I ain't ashamed to tell you my name, mister, and neither are my friends. I'm Judd Whitehorn, and this man closest to me is

Wiley Kelman. The other one is Ed Colter. Feel better now?"

"I'll feel better when you and your pals are gone. Now get out of here!"

"Wait a minute, Britt," said Mary, rising to her feet. "I want to ask them something."

"Ask away," Whitehorn said.

"I know every soldier at Fort Gibson. My father is Dr. Robert Miles, and I am his nurse. We live right there at the fort. I've never seen you three before."

"Well, that's because we were just assigned to Fort Gibson two weeks ago. We ain't been sick, so you'd have no reason to know us. We heard about this weddin', and that the groom was part Cherokee. So we decided to come and tell the bride what we think about a white woman marryin' an Indian. So, now you've been told."

"Okay, Private Whitehorn, you've had your say," Britt said. "Now get out of here before I arrest the three of you and put you in jail."

The huge man ejected a profane oath, took a step closer to Britt, and swung his fist.

The women gasped as Britt dodged the blow and landed a right hook to the jaw that slammed Whitehorn to the ground.

While the big man was trying to get up, Wiley Kelman dashed to Britt, fists flying. Britt avoided the fists and snapped a left hook to Kelman's temple. The young private's head whipped to the side, and he crumpled to the ground.

At the same time, Ed Colter headed for Britt, swearing at him, but John Ross stepped in front of him, pointing a finger. "You stay out of it!"

Colter doubled up a fist, but before he could swing it at John, Britt caught him by the arm, spun him around, and landed a powerful blow to the chin that slammed him to the ground.

Both Colter and Kelman were lying motionless on the ground as Whitehorn got to his feet, roared like a wild beast, and rumbled toward Britt.

Cherokee Rose and Mary were clinging to each other, and John looked on wide-eyed as Britt adeptly avoided a fist and punched Whitehorn in the stomach, followed by a bone-shattering wallop to the jaw. The big man's knees buckled, and he fell to the ground, out cold.

Kelman and Colter were just beginning to come to as Cherokee Rose dashed to her husband's side and Mary ran to John.

"Oh, Britt, I did not realize you could punch so hard!" Cherokee Rose said.

"It makes me mad when foul-mouthed men swear in front of ladies." Britt reached inside his coat and pulled a short-barreled .38 revolver from its holster, and turned to John.

"Hold this gun on these troublemakers. I'll run to our cabin and get some handcuffs and be right back."

When Britt returned, all three of the privates were conscious and sitting on the ground with John Ross standing over them, holding the gun on them.

Britt arrested them for disturbing the peace and handcuffed them with their hands behind their backs. He had the Rosses escort Cherokee Rose to the Claiborne cabin while he took the troublemakers to the police station, told Captain Chinando what they had done, and had them locked up.

The next morning, Captain Chinando assigned an officer to accompany Officer Claiborne as he took the handcuffed soldiers to Fort Gibson. When General Austin Danford learned what the guilty trio had done, he had them dishonorably discharged from the army and sent out of Indian Territory.

Just over four weeks after the Ross wedding, early on Tuesday morning, April 14, Cherokee Rose kissed her husband before he mounted up on Blackie to go on his regular patrol.

Britt held her in his arms and looked down into her soft eyes. "I wish it wasn't so far to Fort Gibson so you could have Dr. Miles deliver the baby instead of Sakah and Lareena doing it."

"Those women have been midwives for over twenty years. They know what they are doing."

"I know, but I have to admit I've been brooding about every known complication associated with childbirth, and I can't help but wonder if Sakah and Lareena know how to handle those complications."

Cherokee Rose raised up on her tiptoes and kissed her husband's cheek. "Darling, the Lord will take care of the baby and me. Everything will be all right."

Britt smiled and said, "You're right, honey. I shouldn't be such a worrywart."

He kissed her, swung into the saddle, told her he loved her, and put Blackie in motion.

Less than half an hour had passed when Cherokee Rose was bending over the washtub in the kitchen. Suddenly, a sharp pain stabbed her in the middle of her lower back. She let out a small groan, straightened up, and rubbed her back where it hurt.

The pain subsided quickly, so she again bent over the washtub, scrubbing the laundry on the scrub board. She thought of the false labor pains she had experienced in the past few days. From what the two midwives had told her, she would know when it was real labor.

Cherokee Rose went on doing the wash. When the clothes had been rinsed and were ready to be hung up on the clothesline behind the cabin, she felt a stab in her lower back again. But this time the pain was stronger, and she gasped at the magnitude of it.

Maybe I should go sit down and rest. I wonder if this is the real thing. It is certainly near my time, and it is different than the other pains.

She sat at the kitchen table, and another pain stabbed her back. This time she felt her abdomen grow taut with it. She drew a short breath, rubbing her abdomen.

Yes. This is the real thing. I am sure of it. Oh, little one, I will soon hold you in my arms.

As she rose from the chair, another pain just like it came, causing her to let out a tiny cry. Cherokee Rose made her way out the back door and onto the porch. She saw her neighbor hanging up her wash and called out, "Majeena! Majeena!"

The forty-year-old woman looked up and saw Cherokee Rose bent over, gripping the railing. She ran toward the Claiborne cabin, and as she drew up to the porch, she said, "Oh, honey, is it time?"

"Yes."

Majeena stepped up on the porch and gripped Cherokee Rose by the shoulders, looking into her pain-filled eyes.

"Let's get you inside to your bed," Majeena said.

Cherokee Rose could only nod her head.

With an arm tight around her shoulders, Majeena guided Cherokee Rose inside the cabin to the main bedroom and helped her sit on the edge of the bed. "You sit right here, honey, and I will get my son to go for the midwives. Do not move. I will be right back."

Majeena hurried away, and Cherokee Rose kneaded her abdomen with her hands and talked quietly to her unborn child. "It will not be long now, little one. We can hardly wait to see you and hold you. You are our gift from God, and you will always be loved by your father and mother, your grandfather, your great-grandparents, and Aunt Tarbee. Just be patient, little one, and soon you will be in your mother's arms."

Majeena was gone only a matter of minutes, and when she came through the back door of the Claiborne cabin and headed for the bedroom, she could hear Cherokee Rose talking to her baby. A smile crossed Majeena's face as she recalled doing the same thing with her son before he was born.

Majeena hurried into the bedroom and said, "My dear, let us get you undressed and into a comfortable gown, then into that bed."

She quickly unbuttoned and removed Cherokee Rose's doeskin dress. The petticoats were next, and soon, after more spasms of pain, the expectant mother was clad in a soft cotton gown. Majeena placed two pillows under her head as the pains came closer and closer together.

As hard as Cherokee Rose tried, she was unable to keep from moaning as each pain became stronger and lasted longer.

When midwives Sakah and Lareena arrived, carrying a pan and a bucket of water, they saw in a glance that Majeena had things well in order. There were washcloths and towels at the bedside, a diaper, and a small blanket.

Majeena held Cherokee Rose's hand as the midwives went to work. Sakah rinsed out a cloth in the cool water and bathed Cherokee Rose's face.

"Oh, that feels so good," the straining mother said between gasps for air. "I—I wish Britt was here."

Suddenly the strongest contraction yet assaulted her.

"Push, honey," Lareena said.

Cherokee Rose closed her eyes and pushed with all her might, and taking a deep breath, she pushed again.

Abruptly, a lusty cry came from her newborn baby, and she

relaxed as Sakah said, "Sweet little mother, you have a perfect little boy! And a noisy one, too!"

As the baby continued to cry, Cherokee Rose looked at him in Sakah's arms and said, "That is the most beautiful sound in all the world!"

"Just another moment and I will have you all cleaned up," Lareena said. "Sakah will clean up your little boy. Then you two can be together."

Moments later, a small bundle wrapped in the soft blanket was placed in Cherokee Rose's arms as she sat up with her back supported by pillows against the head of the bed. The baby was now quiet.

The happy mother gazed down at her precious infant, and her heart seemed to enlarge so it could encompass the little one God had given to her and Britt. She raised him up close to her face and tenderly kissed his chubby cheeks. Then she slowly unfolded the blanket so she could see all of him.

She counted the ten tiny toes and the ten little fingers, then placed soft kisses on them.

After inspecting him thoroughly, Cherokee Rose wrapped him tightly in his blanket and snuggled him close to her heart. She closed her tired eyes and sent a silent, heartfelt prayer of thanksgiving to her heavenly Father.

She then thanked the midwives and Majeena for their help.

Sakah patted her cheek. "You are so welcome. Now just relax while we finish cleaning up."

Majeena looked at Cherokee Rose. "Have you and Britt picked out a name for your little son?"

The smiling mother nodded. "We agreed that if the baby was a boy, we would name him Bradley Allen Claiborne."

Cherokee Rose looked down at her little son, and he was already asleep. She closed her eyes and soon fell asleep herself.

When the three women had the bedroom looking good again, they headed for the kitchen. Majeena excused herself, saying she had to get back to hanging up her wash.

The midwives built a fire in the stove and made some tea. As they sat at the kitchen table, sipping tea, Sakah said, "Well, Lareena, another wee one born safe and sound."

"Yes. Thank the Lord for His mercy."

Late that afternoon, Britt Claiborne rode up to his cabin, led Blackie into the small corral where White Star whinnied at them, removed the saddle and bridle, then stepped up onto the back porch and opened the kitchen door.

Walugo, Tarbee, Bando, Nevarra, and Layne and Sylvia Ward were standing there, smiling at him.

"Are we having a party I forgot about?" Britt said.

All of them laughed.

"Where is my sweet wife?"

"She is in the bedroom holding little Bradley Allen Claiborne… and they are both doing fine," Nevarra said.

Britt ran to the bedroom. Tears filled his eyes as he bent down and kissed a smiling Cherokee Rose, who was holding the little baby boy. Bradley Allen Claiborne was awake and looking around.

"Oh, sweetheart, the Lord has been so good! Can I hold him?"

"Of course," she said, lifting the baby toward his father.

Britt took little Bradley Allen into his arms and studied his features closely. "He looks a whole lot like me, don't you think?"

At that moment, the rest of the family came into the bedroom with the Wards following, and they all told him how they had agreed that his little son looked like him.

Britt bent down close to Cherokee Rose and whispered something.

She nodded and said, "Yes, darling, that would be wonderful."

Britt then said to the preacher, "Pastor, Bradley's mother and I want to dedicate him to the Lord. Would you please lead us in a prayer of dedication?"

Layne Ward smiled. "I would be most honored to do so."

He took the baby into his arms and held him close as heads were bowed for the special occasion.

nineteen

ome two and a half years passed.

On Tuesday, October 26, 1841, Officer Britt Claiborne arrived home from his usual day on patrol, and when he guided Blackie around to the rear of the cabin, he saw Cherokee Rose standing at the small corral behind the cabin with Bradley in her arms. Mother and child were dressed warmly in the cool autumn air. She was holding her little son up to White Star so he could pet the mare's long face.

When Cherokee Rose heard the hoofbeats behind her, she turned and smiled at her husband. "Hello, darling. How did your day go?"

"Just fine," Britt said as he slid from the saddle. "My partner and I only had to arrest one man today. He's in jail for stealing a farmer's hand tools."

Little Bradley took his attention from the mare and reached toward his father. "Papa!"

Britt took him from his mother and said, "Howdy, son! You really like horses, don't you?"

Bradley nodded, grinning. "Uh-huh. Like horses."

"You know what I think our son wants to be when he grows up?" Cherokee Rose said.

"What?"

"A police officer like his papa. You know, who rides patrol on a horse."

Britt kissed his son's cheek. "Well, it would make your papa mighty proud, Bradley. But we'll have to wait and see what the Lord has planned for you."

Britt noticed a sparkle in his wife's eyes as she said, "Well, we will have to wait for the Lord to do the same with Bradley's little sister. I expect, though, that she will be a wife and mother."

Britt stared at her with widened eyes. "Are...are you telling me—"

"Yes, darling! Bradley is going to have a little sister, and *you* are going to have a little daughter."

With his free arm, Britt pulled her close and kissed her. "When is this little girl due?"

"Late May or early June."

"And just how do you know it's a girl?"

"Oh, just a mother's accurate intuition."

"Well, I sure hope you're right! And I suppose you have her named already."

"Well-l-l-l...I sort of thought Elizabeth Ann would be a nice name. Elizabeth Ann Claiborne. Does that sound all right to you?"

"I like it. Elizabeth Ann. You did well, sweetheart. But...what if somehow Bradley gets a little brother instead?"

Cherokee Rose snickered. "Trust me, husband of mine. I just *know* it is a girl."

Britt led Blackie into the corral as Cherokee Rose carried Bradley into the cabin to start supper. Britt couldn't help singing a happy tune while removing the saddle and bridle.

On a Sunday morning the following June, Cherokee Rose gave birth to a healthy baby girl with the aid of midwives Sakah and Lareena. Britt was there and was able to watch the midwives deliver his little daughter.

"You do so well bringing babies into the world," Sakah said as she placed the tiny bundle in Cherokee Rose's arms. "I hope you have many more children."

The happy mother looked up at Sakah and smiled. "Well, if the Lord wills it, we would love to have more children. Little Bradley has been such a blessing."

In the parlor, Britt was tickling his son when Lareena came in and said, "Mr. Claiborne, mother and baby are ready for you to come back now. I will bring Bradley. You go ahead."

Britt thanked her and hurried to the bedroom. He bent down, placed a soft kiss on Cherokee Rose's cheek, then kissed his new daughter's downy head.

Sakah looked on and smiled as he said, "I sure do love these two women in my life."

Lareena came in leading Bradley by the hand, and when the boy saw his mother holding the baby, he ran up, saying he wanted to see his little sister.

Britt picked him up and held him so he could get a good look at her. At the same time, the midwives told the Claibornes that they needed to be going. Both Britt and Cherokee Rose expressed their deep appreciation for their work, and when Britt offered to pay them, as usual they both refused.

When the midwives were gone, Britt helped Bradley up onto the bed so he could sit beside his mother, then said, "Now, it's Papa's turn to hold little Elizabeth Ann."

Britt held the baby girl in his arms, kissed both chubby cheeks, then ran his gaze over her little face. After studying her features for several seconds, he looked down at Cherokee Rose and said, "I can't get over how much this baby looks like a full-blooded Cherokee. Her skin, her eyes, and her hair are as dark as any Cherokee I've ever seen."

"I noticed that, too," Cherokee Rose said. "She could easily pass for a full-blood."

Britt smiled at the baby, then looked back at his wife. "And have you noticed that she resembles her mother as much as Bradley resembles his father?"

"That was the next thing I was going to point out. She sure does look like me. Oh, I am so proud!"

"Well, she's beautiful, all right. Just like her mother."

Cherokee Rose blushed. "Darling, I have been thinking about something ever since Sakah put her in my arms. I was going to talk to you about it."

"Mm-hmm?"

"Since…since she looks like a full-blooded Indian, I think we should give her an Indian name instead of calling her Elizabeth Ann."

A slow grin spread over Britt's face. "I think that would be excellent. Do you have a name in mind?"

"How about Summer Dawn?"

"Oh, I *like* that! Summer Dawn. Yes!"

In the third week of August 1843, at the Fort Gibson medical office, Mary Ross was doing paperwork at her desk when she heard footsteps on the wooden porch. She looked up to see Chief Bando and two young Cherokee men coming through the door. The young men were carrying Chief Sequoyah, whose face was pallid.

As Mary rose from her chair, Bando said, "Chief Sequoyah is having severe pains in his chest, Mrs. Ross. Is the doctor in?"

"Yes, he is with a patient in the examining room. Let's get Chief Sequoyah back there quickly so my father can look at him."

Mary guided them to one of the examining tables, and as Sequoyah was being placed on the table, Mary hurried to her father.

Dr. Robert Miles quickly finished with the other patient and hurried to the examining table where Sequoyah lay, clenching his teeth and gripping his chest as the pains continued.

Bando and the young men looked on as Dr. Miles spoke softly to the aging chief while he used his stethoscope to listen to his heart. Mary held Sequoyah's hand.

After listening to several different places on Sequoyah's chest and back, Dr. Miles looked at Bando and the young men and said, "I detect a critically irregular heartbeat. I want to keep him here for observation for a couple of days."

Bando nodded. "All right, Doctor. We will come back day after tomorrow."

"Fine. Make it in the afternoon if you can."

Bando laid a hand on Sequoyah's shoulder and said, "You are in God's hands, dear friend. And you are in the good hands of an excellent physician. We will be praying for you."

Sequoyah nodded and whispered, "Thank you."

"I am going to give you a sedative now, Chief," the doctor said as Mary led the three men back toward the office.

"How is President Ross doing?" Chief Bando asked Mary.

"Just over three weeks ago he headed for Washington to spend some time with President Tyler. His intention is to make life better for the Indians of Indian Territory by working with the president and other government leaders."

Bando smiled. "That sounds like John Ross."

"Doesn't it, though?" Mary said, chuckling. "I expect him to be home in about four or five days."

"Well, God bless him for his efforts," Bando said as he and the two young men headed for the door.

When Bando and the two young Cherokee men returned late in the afternoon two days later, they had Pastor Layne Ward with them.

Mary Ross was talking to a soldier who was wearing a sling on his right arm as they stepped through the door. She finished her conversation with the soldier, and when he headed toward the door, Mary greeted the Indians, then said, "Pastor Ward, I'm glad you could come along today. The doctor is with Chief Sequoyah right now and is expecting you. I'll take you to the back room."

Mary led the four men into the back room where her father stood over Sequoyah, who lay on a bed.

"My patient here is ready for you to take him home," Dr. Miles said after greeting the men.

"So he is doing better, Doctor?" Bando asked.

Sequoyah managed a weak smile.

"Somewhat." Dr. Miles picked up a glass bottle with a dry white powder in it. "I'm giving him this bottle of acetylsalicylic acid to take home. We gave him two doses the day you brought him in and two doses yesterday. I've shown him how to mix the powder with water and explained that he is to take it twice a day. He hasn't had any chest pains for about twenty-four hours now. I told him if he has any more, he is to take a dose right away. Other than this, there's nothing I can do for him."

"How long will this bottle last him, Doctor?" Bando asked.

"About two weeks. I'm running a bit low on it, but I'm having more shipped in from my supplier in Little Rock. It'll be here long before Chief Sequoyah runs out of what he has."

"All right," Bando said. "I will check with you for more of the powder when Chief Sequoyah's supply is getting low."

Dr. Miles nodded. "I've made it clear to Chief Sequoyah that he should be very careful not to overexert himself. He must get plenty of rest."

Pastor Ward looked down at the aging chief. "You do understand what the doctor is saying, don't you?"

Sequoyah managed a thin smile. "I do, Pastor."

Mary leaned over the patient. "Promise me that you'll get plenty of rest."

Sequoyah met her gaze. "I promise."

"Dr. Miles, before we take Chief Sequoyah home, I would like to pray for him," Pastor Ward said.

"Of course. Go right ahead."

Mary held Sequoyah's hand as the pastor led in prayer. When Pastor Ward finished his prayer, Mary was wiping tears, as was the ailing chief.

One starlit night a few days after Chief Sequoyah had returned to his cabin—which was a few doors down the path from Chief Bando's cabin—he sat on the porch, gazing at the glittering sky.

Sequoyah was used to solitude in his life. For most of his adult years, he had lived alone. He enjoyed being with other people, but mostly he enjoyed the peace and quiet of his solitary way of living.

He yawned and decided it was time to move inside and go to bed. As he strained to lift himself from the chair, suddenly there was sharp pain in his chest. It was so severe, it took his breath, and he stared into the night with blank-faced astonishment.

He shuffled his way into the cabin and headed for the kitchen, where he had left a lantern burning. He had already taken his two doses of acetylsalicylic acid that day, but recalling that Dr. Miles had told him to take a dose if he had heart pains, he entered the kitchen, mixed the powder and water with shaky hands, and drank it down.

He shuffled into the parlor, lit the lantern, and with a sigh, sat down on his overstuffed chair. He sat there, feeling his heart pounding in his chest. It was getting worse, and he could hardly breathe.

Sequoyah sat there for some time, but he could tell that the medication was not working. His heart was beating like the frantic wings of a trapped bird. He told himself there was nothing else that could be done for him. Dr. Robert Miles was too far away to be of help.

Chief Sequoyah gasped for breath as he looked at his small inelegant desk next to the wall by the window. "Lord," he said in a whisper, "I have one thing to do before You take me to be with You. Please allow it."

He struggled to his feet, shuffled to the desk, and sat down on the chair. The pain was worsening as Sequoyah opened a drawer and took out a pen and an ink bottle and a sheet of paper. He dipped the pen into the bottle and used his left hand to steady his right hand as he wrote:

I am so glad that my Cherokee people have found their new home and are happy and content in Indian Territory. The stars are bright tonight!

Sequoyah read over his words and nodded in satisfaction. He left the paper on the desk, struggled to his feet once more, and slowly made his way to his bedroom. Lying down on the cornhusk mattress, he let his mind wander back over his life. He thought of the day when the white missionary showed him from the Bible how to receive the Lord Jesus as his Saviour, and he recalled the joy that filled his soul when he did so.

Another fierce pain lanced through his chest. He gasped, then turned his head and looked out the window beside the bed. The stars were shining brightly in the night sky, and he gazed at their singular beauty.

A frail smile formed on his lips, a deep sigh escaped his mouth, and Chief Sequoyah's fragile heart beat one last time.

The next morning, Chief Bando went as usual to Sequoyah's cabin to check on him. When there was no answer to his knock, Bando opened the door and went inside. There was absolute silence.

Bando figured the chief must still be in bed. When he was moving past the desk, he saw the pen and ink and the sheet of paper. He paused to read what the chief had written.

With the words echoing in his mind, Bando made his way to the bedroom and found what he had expected.

Pastor Layne Ward was summoned to the cabin, and he wiped tears when he read the note. Chief Bando said he would send a rider to let President John Ross know that Chief Sequoyah had died.

At Sequoyah's funeral, John Ross stood beside the grave and reminded the huge crowd of Chief Sequoyah's delight over the happiness and prosperity of his Cherokee people in their new land. John read to them what Sequoyah had penned just before his death. Many tears were shed in the crowd as they repeated to each other, "The stars are bright tonight."

Layne Ward brought a heartfelt message to the crowd, giving a clear explanation of the gospel of Jesus Christ. He spoke of Chief Sequoyah's hard work in translating the Bible into the Cherokee language so the Cherokee people could learn of the Saviour and go to heaven when their lives were over.

At the end of his message, Pastor Ward looked toward heaven and said, "I will tell you this, my dear friends—when night falls at the close of this day, we can all look up there and say, 'The stars are bright tonight!'"

As the months passed, each day when it was time for Officer Britt Claiborne to arrive home from his long day on patrol, little Bradley Allen would go to the front window of the cabin to watch for his father. When the boy would catch sight of his father on the big black horse, he would squeal with excitement. This would bring Cherokee Rose with her baby daughter in her arms, and mother and children would step out onto the front porch to welcome Britt home. Britt found his son and daughter to be more of a blessing than he had ever imagined.

One night after the children were in bed asleep, Britt and Cherokee Rose sat down together on the sofa in the parlor and talked about how much they loved Bradley and Summer.

A wistful look captured Cherokee Rose's eyes as she said, "Oh, darling, I hope the Lord gives us more children."

Britt grinned at her and pulled her closer to him. "Summer is not quite two years old. We have plenty of time for more babies."

"That's my point. Summer is almost two and growing like a weed. I need another wee one to put in the cradle!"

Britt kissed her cheek. "You are really something, Mrs. Claiborne. More precious children would be fine with me, but we must be patient. In God's timing, He will send more babies to us if that is His will."

She smiled and said softly, "You are right, Britt. And we must always be grateful for what we have here and now. We will give the two sweet babies the Lord has given us all the love we possibly can, and we will raise them to love and serve Him."

Twenty

ne starlit night in September 1844, Britt and Cherokee Rose took Bradley and Summer Dawn to the bubbling stream that ran close to their cabin. Bradley had turned four in April, and Summer Dawn had turned two in June. As they were sitting together on the bank of the stream, Britt placed an arm around his wife and pulled her close. "Honey, I was just thinking about when we soldiers came to North Carolina and ordered the Cherokee people off their land."

She pulled her lips into a thin line and nodded. "That was the darkest day of our lives. We had to leave so much that was dear to us…our homeland."

"I know, but what I was thinking was that through it all, God in His wisdom brought about so many good things. If He had not allowed it, you and I would never have met. And your Cherokee people would never have been able to enjoy what they have here."

A smile formed on Cherokee Rose's lips. She met Britt's gaze in the light of the stars and said, "We wouldn't have these two precious children either. The Lord has been so good to us. And He has been so good to the Cherokee people. I know they all love this land."

Cherokee Rose put a hand to her mouth and sniffed. "My people went through some deep and dark valleys on that Trail of Tears. We lost so many loved ones and friends, but the Lord has given us so many blessings in this new place that we have learned to call *home*."

"I was reading just today in my Bible where Peter said, 'But the God of all grace, who hath called us unto his eternal glory by Christ Jesus, after that ye have suffered a while, make you perfect, stablish, strengthen, settle you.' That is exactly what He has done for the Christians in the Cherokee Nation. After you had suffered a while, He settled you and gave you more than you ever had before."

"What a marvelous verse!" Cherokee Rose said. "And how wonderful it is to be settled in this beautiful place the Lord has given us as our home."

"Praise the Lord!" Britt said. "The stars are bright tonight!"

"Indeed they are, darling. Because the Lord gave me you and my precious children and because we Cherokees finally found a place to call home!"

One cold wintry night in January 1846, Chief Bando lay in his bed, a debilitating, racking cough consuming him. He had been sick for a few days and now was worse. Nevarra left him long enough to make her way through the deep snow to the Claiborne cabin.

When Britt and Cherokee Rose went with Nevarra and saw how ill Bando was, Britt hurried to Walugo's cabin, awakened him, told him how sick Bando was, and asked if he would take Bando to Dr. Robert Miles at Fort Gibson. Walugo understood that Britt had pressing business as the new head police officer, having replaced retiring Captain Chinando, and could not leave his office.

By sunup, Tarbee was staying with Bradley and Summer Dawn while Cherokee Rose accompanied her grandmother and her father as he drove the wagon through the snow toward Fort Gibson. Both women were in the bed of the wagon with Bando, making sure he stayed as warm as possible.

That evening, when Britt arrived at the Claiborne cabin, Tarbee told him that Bando was back home and in bed. Dr. Miles had done what he could for him, but gave little hope that Bando would live.

Britt went to the Bando cabin, where Nevarra and Cherokee Rose told him that their loved one's condition was deteriorating almost hourly, and most of the time he slept, waking only to sip on broth and hot tea. Pastor Layne Ward had just been there and had prayed over Bando, asking the Lord not to allow him to suffer.

Britt told Cherokee Rose that Tarbee had supper waiting for him. He would go back home and eat, then return.

When Britt was gone, Cherokee Rose sat on one side of her

grandfather's bed, with her grandmother on the other side. Each of them held one of his hands. The two women were weary and sat in silence, their eyes fixed on Bando. Both knew he would have to be awakened in another hour or so and given more broth and tea.

Suddenly, Bando surprised them by awaking and looking at them. His hands gripped theirs tightly. Before either woman could ask if he wanted anything, Bando coughed and said clearly, "I am going home. I am going home."

His eyes closed and his hands went slack.

With tears in her eyes, Cherokee Rose looked at her grandmother. Tears coursed down Nevarra's wrinkled cheeks, but at the same time, a beautiful smile glowed on her face. "Cherokee Rose, God gave us a place to call home here on earth, but your grandfather has now gone to be with Him in his 'long home' for all eternity. He is not suffering anymore."

In June of 1847, Nevarra became very ill. She had been quite lonely without her mate of so many years, and soon her heart was giving her trouble. She was taken to Dr. Miles, who gave her medicine for her heart, but she had only been back home less than a week when she lay on her bed, dying.

Cherokee Rose had been at her side day and night, with Tarbee and another Indian woman watching over Bradley and Summer Dawn.

Late one afternoon, as Cherokee Rose sat at her grandmother's side, Nevarra suddenly jerked, gasped, and put a hand to her chest.

"Oh, Grandmother!" Cherokee Rose said, rising to her feet and taking hold of Nevarra's shoulders. "What can I do for you?"

Nevarra looked up at her with weary eyes and said, "Nothing, dear. I am going home."

Cherokee Rose's eyes filled with tears. "Oh, Grandmother, I—"

"Please do not grieve for me, sweet girl. I want to go to heaven and see my wonderful Jesus. And…and to be with your grandfather. I will be happy in my eternal home."

Nevarra closed her eyes, relaxed, and a smile curved her lips as she let out her last breath.

Cherokee Rose wept for a few minutes. Then wiping tears from her cheeks, she said aloud, "Yes, my grandparents are together again. They are with Jesus. They are really home at last."

Time moved on. In 1859, at forty-two years of age, Britt Claiborne was promoted to chief of police in Indian Territory when Chief Yasson stepped aside because of ill health. Britt, Cherokee Rose, and their teenage children moved to Tahlequah, purchased a larger cabin than they had before, and Britt settled into his new job. Only a few weeks later, Walugo moved to Tahlequah also, saying he wanted to be close to his daughter, son-in-law, and grand-children.

As president of the United Cherokee Nation, John Ross often traveled to Washington DC, and Mary, who had retired from her nursing job with her father, always went with him. In the last week of July 1866, John and Mary Ross traveled once again to the nation's capital to do business with President Andrew Johnson, who gave John time with him in the Oval Office each day while Mary remained at their hotel. On this trip, there was old business to discuss for a few days, then John had something new he wanted President Johnson to consider.

On Wednesday morning, August 1, President Ross sat down with President Johnson, who said, "Well, my friend, today you're going to present the new concept for relations between your government and mine, right?"

Ross opened his leather case and said, "Yes, sir. I believe this will have your absolute approval, Mr. President."

Suddenly, John Ross closed his eyes, shook his head, dropped his case on the floor, and fell from his chair. Johnson bent over him, listening to his ragged breathing, then dashed out of the Oval Office to tell his secretary to fetch the White House nurse.

Ross lay on the floor and felt something cold surging up in his head. He could hear himself mumbling, but he could not see. Seconds later, Johnson was kneeling over him, and to Ross, his voice sounded distant.

Sarah Wilson, the White House nurse, entered the room, carrying her black leather medical bag, and knelt beside Johnson. While Johnson told her what had happened, she started examining John Ross. She listened to his heart with a stethoscope and checked his pulse at the wrist. While she was forcing his eyelids open and noting his bloodshot eyes, he gasped, shook all over, and went limp.

Feeling for a pulse in his neck, Sarah looked at President Johnson and said, "He is dead, Mr. President. A massive stroke killed him. Look at how his face is drawn up on the left side."

Johnson nodded and sighed. "Mrs. Ross is at the Pennsylvania Avenue Hotel. Will you go and tell her what has happened? You can explain it much better than I can."

"Certainly, sir."

"I'll send Lester Morton with you. She's met Lester before. Bring Mrs. Ross here to the Oval Office, and Mrs. Johnson and I will do what we can to comfort her. "

At her room in the Pennsylvania Avenue Hotel, Mary Ross was seated on a sofa, reading a newspaper from April 15, 1865, which told of President Abraham Lincoln's assassination.

There was a knock at the door.

Mary laid the paper down and went to the door. When she opened it, she saw a woman clad in white and President Johnson's aide, Lester Morton, at her side. By the look on their faces, she sensed that something was amiss.

"Hello, Mr. Morton," she said. "Is something wrong?"

Morton swallowed hard. "Mrs. Ross, this lady is the White House nurse. Her name is Sarah Wilson. May we come in?"

Mary's voice was shaky as she said, "Yes, of course."

Sarah took Mary by the hand and said softly, "Let's sit down."

"What is it? Has something happened to my husband?"

Sarah guided Mary to the room's small sofa and sat down with her. "Mrs. Ross, your husband…well, he had a massive stroke while he was in President Johnson's office. He…he died while I was examining him."

Mary became motionless as stone. Her face took on a chalky whiteness as she stammered, "John is…dead?"

"Yes. I'm so sorry. He went quickly, Mrs. Ross. He suffered very little pain, I assure you."

Tears filled Mary's eyes and began to stream down her face.

Lester stood beside the sofa and placed a hand on Mary's

shoulder. "Mrs. Ross, my heart goes out to you. Is there anything I can do for you? Is there someone here in Washington I can get to come and be with you?"

"No, Mr. Morton," she said, wiping her tears. "Thank you for offering. I…I want to go to my husband's body."

"Of course. Sarah and I will take you there. We have a White House buggy waiting outside."

Lester and Sarah escorted Mary Ross from the hotel, each holding a hand, and guided her to the buggy. Mary stopped before climbing into the buggy and glanced around her. The street was busy with shoppers on the boardwalks and horse-drawn buggies and wagons moving along the busy thoroughfare. She looked up at the sun, which was shining in a cobalt blue sky, and said, "Isn't it odd how this world goes right on all around us when our own world has fallen apart?"

Neither Sarah nor Lester spoke, but both helped her up into the buggy.

When they reached the White House, Mary was guided to the Oval Office, where President and Mrs. Johnson met her, speaking words of condolence.

John's body had been placed on an ornate overstuffed sofa and covered with a sheet. When Mary saw it, a soft gasp escaped her lips, and she quickly put her hand to her mouth to muffle the sound.

Mrs. Johnson and Sarah guided Mary toward the sofa. Lester placed a straight-backed wooden chair beside the sofa, and the two women helped Mary sit down. With trembling hands, she took hold of the sheet and pulled it down, exposing her husband's face. Once again, tears ran down her cheeks.

Sarah leaned close and said, "Mrs. Ross, we will leave the room and give you some privacy to mourn your loss."

Mary looked up at her. "Thank you. My husband knew Christ as Saviour, and I know he is in heaven. But it is still hard to let him go."

"I understand," Sarah said. "We'll be back in a little while."

When the other four had left the room, Mary reached out and lightly stroked her husband's dear, familiar face, then pulled the sheet farther down and entwined her fingers with those of John's right hand. In a soft voice, she said, "John, when I thought the rest of my life was to be lived alone, you came into it, and nothing has been the same since. After losing my first husband, I thought I would remain a widow. But you walked into my life, and we learned together how to rebuild our lives. I know you are with the Lord, and I cannot wish you back into this old world. But my life will never be the same without you."

Tears still streamed down her cheeks as she stared at John's face, committing it to memory. Then she stood up and placed a tender kiss on his cheek. After pulling the sheet back up and covering the body, Mary squared her shoulders and walked toward the door.

At that moment, President Johnson, his wife, nurse, and aide came through the door.

"I want to thank you for how kind you've been to me," Mary said.

"It's the least we could do, Mrs. Ross," President Johnson said. "I want you to know that I have made arrangements for you to take your husband's body back to Indian Territory so he can be buried in his homeland."

A tiny smile graced her lips. "Thank you, Mr. President. I know this would mean a lot to John, and it certainly means a lot to me."

twenty-one

riday, July 3, 1885, was a hot, humid day in Missouri as Wilbur Schofield drove his hay wagon along a dusty road with his wife, Emma, at his side. It was early afternoon as the Schofield wagon passed farm after farm.

Wilbur lifted his straw hat and wiped perspiration from his forehead. "I think we've come close to five miles since we left Joplin, honey. Wouldn't you say?"

Emma patted her face with a handkerchief and nodded. "I would say so. Mr. Wilkins did say the Parker farm was five miles *south* of Joplin, didn't he?"

"Yes, and we've been moving south ever since we pulled out of town. We gotta be getting close."

Emma pointed at a farm up ahead on the right. "Maybe that's it. See all those haystacks?"

"Yeah. Mr. Wilkins did say that the Parker farm has more haystacks than any other farm in the area. I guess with a hundred and seventy acres of alfalfa, they'd have plenty of hay stacked up by now, even though there's a third cutting yet to be harvested."

Wilbur put the two horses to a trot, and as they drew near to the spot where a wagon path met the road, he pulled rein, and they both saw the sign on a fence post: *Craig and Gloria Parker.*

"This is it," Emma said.

Wilbur drove the horses along the path that led toward the farmstead. As they drew near the white, two-story house, the Schofields saw a tall, slender young man dressed in blue overalls, gray shirt, and straw hat with a dark brown band talking to a young woman, whom they presumed was his wife. The couple noticed the arriving hay wagon and headed toward it.

"Hello! May we help you?" the young man said as Wilbur drew rein.

"Yes, I'm Wilbur Schofield, and this is my wife, Emma. We were told in town that we could buy a wagon load of alfalfa hay from you. We just moved onto a farm about a mile north of Joplin, and we need some hay for our livestock. We're originally from Nebraska."

"That's what we're in the hay business for. I'm Craig and this is my wife, Gloria."

"Pleased to meet you both. How long've you had the farm?" Wilbur asked.

"A year and a half. We've been married for three years. Came here from Iowa. You want a whole load?"

"Sure do," Wilbur said.

"Okay. Looks like it'll stack about eight feet high with those frames at the front and back of the bed, so considering the width of the wagon, I'll let you have a full load for twelve dollars."

Wilbur grinned. "Sounds fair enough to me. Would you help me load it?"

"Sure." Craig pointed toward the long rows of haystacks. "We'll take it from the first stack on that row right over there."

It was midafternoon when Craig and Gloria watched the Schofields drive away with their load of hay.

Craig turned to Gloria. "I need to drive the wagon to town and pick up those tools I had Benny order for me at the hardware store. I'll be back in a couple of hours."

Gloria smiled. "All right. Ah…are you remembering that this evening I'm going to the revival meeting at the church in Joplin that Harold and Diana Mitchell go to?"

"Mm-hmm. I remember." Craig wished their closest neighbors lived somewhere else, but he refrained from saying so.

She put a pleading look on her pretty face. "Would you reconsider your refusal to go with us? I'd really like to have you at my side. The evangelist is J. Wilbur Chapman, who is quite well-known, and Harold and Diana told me he's an excellent preacher. Will you go with me? Pretty please?"

Craig shook his head. "I don't want to hurt your feelings, honey, but I'm just not interested in all that fanatical religious stuff the Mitchells are involved with. I don't believe all that Bible rigmarole. It just doesn't interest me."

"Well, if you're not back from town in time for supper, I'll leave it on the table for you. The Mitchells are picking me up at six so we can get good seats."

"I'll be back in time for supper."

Moments later, Gloria stood on the front porch of their farm-house, and tears filled her eyes as she watched her husband drive away in his wagon.

At the same time Craig Parker was leaving the outskirts of Joplin after picking up his new tools, Evan Koehler was at his desk in the open area near the tellers' cages at the Joplin National Bank down-town. It was almost closing time, and Koehler began placing the papers he had been working on in a folder when he heard the front door of the bank swing open and a male voice bellow, "All right, everybody! Get your hands in the air!"

Koehler looked up to see a tall, slender man dressed in overalls and a gray shirt, holding a cocked revolver. He wore a straw hat with a dark brown band and a black bandanna for a mask. The robber waved his gun at the few customers who stood in line at the tellers' windows and growled, "Every one of you, get down on the floor and lie facedown!"

When this order was obeyed, the masked man stepped up to the closest teller's window and said to the woman whose face was white with fear, "Clean out all the drawers at these windows and put the money in one of those canvas bags there on the counter!"

He ordered the other tellers, vice president Evan Koehler, and a secretary who sat at a desk near his to get down on the floor.

A minute later, the robber ran out of the bank, carrying the canvas bag packed with currency. The robbery had taken all of four minutes.

As employees and customers were getting to their feet, Evan said, "Everybody, stay right here! I'm going to get the sheriff. He'll want to hear every one of you describe that masked robber."

At the sheriff's office, which was less than a block from the bank, Sheriff Edgar Warren and two of his deputies, Wade Handley and Lou Alton, were looking over some wanted posters that had just arrived from the U.S. Marshal's office in St. Louis. They looked up to see a white-faced Evan Koehler come through the door.

"Sheriff, the bank just got robbed! It was a masked man, alone. He got away with a lot of money. I don't know how much yet, but it has to have been a large amount."

"Can you give us a description of him, Evan?" the sheriff asked.

"Yes, but I told all of the bank employees and the customers who were there during the robbery to stay put till I could get you and have them tell you what they saw."

"We'll go talk to them right now. But first, give me your description of him." As he spoke, the sheriff picked up paper and a pencil from his desktop.

"Well, I'd say he was about six feet tall. Slender. He wore a black bandanna over his face. He was in overalls and wore a straw hat."

The sheriff wrote it down. "Could you tell what color his eyes were?"

Koehler shook his head. "Not for sure. Dark. Maybe brown."

The sheriff nodded and wrote it down. "Okay. Let's go, fellas."

Some ten minutes later, Sheriff Warren and Deputies Handley and Alton stood before the group of bank employees and customers who had witnessed the robbery. The bank was now closed for the day.

Sheriff Warren repeated the description Evan Koehler had

given him of the robber, then said, "Can any of you give me more than that?"

"Yes, Sheriff," one of the male customers said. "His eyes were definitely dark brown."

"All right. Anyone else?"

"His straw hat had a dark brown band," one of the female tellers said.

"And he wore a gray shirt," a female customer said.

"Light or dark gray?" Warren asked.

"Light gray."

Everyone nodded their agreement.

Another male customer said, "Sheriff, I don't like to say this, but..." The man cleared his throat. "Well, it's impossible to be positive, but the robber was built exactly like Craig Parker. You know him, don't you? He has a farm south of town a few miles."

"I've met him, yes," Warren said.

"I hadn't thought of it, but the robber was built like Craig," Evan Koehler said. "The bank also has a mortgage on their farm." He rubbed his chin. "And now that I think of it, the robber did walk like Craig."

"And his voice certainly resembled Craig's, even though he spoke gruffly," another male customer said. "And I saw him drive into town in his buggy a while ago."

Deputy Handley looked at the sheriff. "Sounds like we have enough to go after Parker."

Warren nodded. "I would say so."

"Oh, Sheriff," spoke up the female teller who had faced the robber over the counter. "Something else..."

"Mm-hmm?"

"The black bandanna he wore had a thin white fringe around its edges."

Deputy Alton smiled. "Leave it to a lady to notice that."

Craig Parker was no more than two miles out of Joplin when the left front wheel of his wagon began to wobble and make a loud grinding sound. He pulled the team to a halt, then had them pull the wagon slowly into a nearby stand of trees. When he found an open spot, he drew rein.

Craig hopped down from the wagon seat, gripped the iron rim of the wheel, and gave it a shake. He saw instantly that the axle bolt was loose. He reached into the wagon bed and opened his toolbox, took out the wrench that fit the head of the axle bolt, and went to work.

Within a few minutes, Craig had the bolt tightened. He went to the other three wheels and made sure their axle bolts were snug.

"Well, boys, it's fixed," he said to the horses. "We can head on home now."

As Craig stepped to the front wheel to climb into the wagon seat, he heard the thundering hoofbeats of a galloping horse pass by on the road. He looked that direction, but too many trees blocked his view. He shrugged, climbed onto the seat, and guided the horses through the thick stand of trees toward the road. When the wagon cleared the trees and was pulling onto the road, Craig spotted a black bandanna lying at the road's edge.

Funny, he thought, *I didn't notice that bandanna when I pulled in here.*

Craig halted the horses, jumped to the ground, and picked up the bandanna, noticing that it had a thin white fringe around its edges. He stuffed it into his shirt pocket, climbed back onto the wagon seat, and headed for home.

As the Parker farm came into view, Craig pulled his pocket watch from the breast pocket of his overalls and noted that it was ten minutes after six.

He drove the wagon up to the toolshed, placed the new tools inside, then drove the wagon into the barn. He unhitched the horses and put them in the corral with his saddle horse and walked toward the back door of the house. He knew his neighbors were sticklers for always being on time, so he was sure Gloria was already on her way to the church in Joplin with them.

When Craig entered the kitchen, he saw the food on the table, as Gloria had promised. Craig sighed, hung his straw hat on its peg next to the door, and went to the counter by the cupboard where the wash-bowl was kept. He washed his hands, then went to the stove, which was still warm, and poured himself a cup of coffee. He placed the steaming cup by his plate, then pulled out his chair and sat down.

Outside, Sheriff Edgar Warren and Deputies Wade Handley and Lou Alton drew up on their horses to within some thirty yards of the farmhouse and dismounted.

"Both of you go cover the back door," the sheriff said in a low voice as he pulled his Colt .45 revolver from its holster. "I'll knock on the front door."

The two deputies pulled their guns and hurried toward the rear of the house. The sheriff headed for the front porch.

Craig Parker was spooning gravy from a lidded bowl onto his plateful of mashed potatoes when he heard a loud knock at the front door.

"Who could that be?" he said aloud as he scooted his chair back and headed toward the front of the house.

There was a second knock just as he drew up to the door. He pulled it open and was stunned when he saw Sheriff Edgar Warren holding his gun on him with a deep scowl on his face.

"Get your hands in the air, Parker!" the sheriff barked.

Craig's throat went tight as he raised his hands over his head. "Wha–? What are you doing, Sheriff?"

"I'm putting you under arrest, that's what. Come around front, men!" Warren shouted. "I've got my gun on him!"

Craig swallowed hard. "Sheriff, I don't understand. Why am I being arrested?"

"I'm arresting you for robbing the Joplin National Bank just before it closed this afternoon!"

Craig's eyes bulged. "Sheriff, you're making a mistake! I did no such thing! What makes you think it was me?"

As the deputies bounded up onto the front porch of the house, brandishing their guns, Warren said, "You were in town this afternoon, weren't you?"

"Well, yes, but—"

"See there, Sheriff," Deputy Lou Alton said. "Overalls and a gray shirt. Just like the witnesses said."

"What are you talking about?" Craig said, still holding his hands above his head.

"Don't play innocent with us, Parker!" the sheriff said. "Even though you wore a mask, people in the bank identified you, even describing your overalls and gray shirt. I want to see your straw hat."

"What for?"

"The witnesses at the bank robbery described it. Where is it?"

"In the kitchen."

"Let's go."

The three lawmen followed Craig Parker as he led them to the kitchen at the rear of the house. When they stepped into the kitchen, Lou Alton spied the hat hanging next to the back door, dashed to it, and yanked it off the peg.

"See there, Sheriff? Dark brown band! Exactly as the witnesses told us!"

Craig shook his head in disbelief. "Most straw hats have a dark brown band. I'm telling you, Sheriff, I did not rob that bank! My wife and I have a checking account there. The loan on our farm is there. Why would I rob it?"

"I don't know," Warren said. "The witnesses also described your build and the way you walk. With all this other clear evidence… like I said, you're under arrest. Where did you stash the money?"

Craig's face was ashen. He started to say something else when Deputy Handley spotted the tip of the black bandanna that Craig had stuffed into his shirt pocket. He stepped up, yanked it out, and held it up so the sheriff and Alton could get a good look at it.

"Just exactly like that lady teller told us!"

"That's not mine. Sheriff, I tell you it's not mine! I found it on the ground beside the road where I had stopped to work on one of my wagon wheels."

Handley laughed. "You're a liar, Parker!"

"A liar that's going to prison for a long time," the sheriff said. "But if you'll tell us where you stashed the money, it might go better for you at your trial."

Parker's face went red, and the muscles in his jaws tightened. "Sheriff, I'm telling you, I didn't rob that bank! I'm innocent! Sure, there are some coincidences, but I'm telling you the truth. I found that bandanna at the edge of the road after I finished working on my wagon. Come to think of it, I heard a horse gallop by just before I found it. The guy on that galloping horse had to have been the robber!"

The sheriff gave Craig Parker a skeptical look. "Coincidences, all right. But more than coincidences. It was *you* who robbed that bank. Now, I'm asking you for the last time—where did you stash the money?"

A sheen of sweat now coated Craig's face. A tremor of hopelessness pulsed through him. "Sheriff, I'm telling you the truth. I did not rob the bank."

Warren held hot eyes on Parker as he snapped, "Wade! Lou! Handcuff him!"

Wade Handley moved up behind Parker, pulled his arms down behind his waist, and held them there while Lou Alton placed the cuffs on his wrists and snapped them closed.

As the lawmen shoved Craig Parker through the house toward the front door, his mind was a whirlpool of despair.

Later that evening, Gloria Parker rode in the Mitchells' wagon seat next to Diana as they headed home. She wiped happy tears with her handkerchief as she said, "Oh, I'm so glad I walked down the aisle when Mr. Chapman gave the invitation! And I'm so glad your pastor had *you* take me to the altar, Diana. Thank you for leading me to Jesus. My sins have been washed away, and I'm going to heaven when my life here is over!"

Diana hugged her. "Praise the Lord! I'm so happy, Gloria!"

"It's wonderful to know that our names are written in the Lamb's Book of Life like Mr. Chapman preached, isn't it, Gloria?" Harold Mitchell said.

"It sure is! I can hardly wait to tell Craig about the sermon so he'll want his name in that Book, too."

ne day in late October of 1888, Police Chief Britt Claiborne was sitting at the desk in his office when there was a tap on the door. It was the Cherokee police officer on duty in the front office.

"Chief, a Lawrence Kirkland is here to see you. He says you and he are old friends."

"Oh, my, Captain Kirkland and I go back a long ways," the silver-haired chief said. "Please bring him in."

Britt stood to his feet and was moving around in front of his desk when Lawrence Kirkland came through the door. The two came together and shook hands warmly.

"Do you realize that it's been over forty years since you left Fort Gibson?" Britt said. "Where did you get all that gray hair?"

"I was about to ask you the same thing."

Britt chuckled. "It happens, doesn't it?"

"If a person lives long enough, it sure does."

"Well, come in, Captain, and sit down," said Britt, gesturing toward a small overstuffed sofa.

When Kirkland eased onto the sofa, Britt drew up a straight-backed wooden chair and sat down. They talked for a while about Kirkland's transfer from Fort Gibson to Fort Atkinson in Iowa. When that fort was closed down, he retired from the army and bought a farm nearby. The two men then talked about their growing families and got caught up on the latest news about their children and grandchildren and even great-grandchildren.

The two old friends continued to chat about a number of things, including the recent name change of Indian Territory to Oklahoma District that President Grover Cleveland and Congress had instituted. Both speculated for a while what that change was all about. Then Lawrence told Britt he needed to be going. Britt thanked him for stopping by and said he hoped they would soon see each other again.

One day in the third week of January 1889, Mandula, Tahlequah's postmaster, came to Britt Claiborne's office.

"I have a very important letter for you," Mandula said to Britt.

"Must be important if the postmaster delivers it personally," Britt said as Mandula handed him the envelope. "I—" Britt's eyes fastened on the return address in the upper left-hand corner. "It...it's from the new president of the United States, Benjamin Harrison."

"That's why I wanted to make sure I got it to you right away. Well, I must get back to the post office."

Britt thanked Mandula, and as soon as he had gone out the door, Britt sat down at his desk, slit the envelope open with a letter opener, and began to read.

When he finished reading the letter, Britt Claiborne left his office and walked briskly toward the church building in Tahlequah, where he and Cherokee Rose were now members. Layne Ward had died several years before, and a young Cherokee man named Joshudo, who was saved and called to preach under Pastor Ward's ministry, had been sent by Pastor Ward's church to start a new church in Tahlequah. Sylvia Ward had lived almost a year longer than her husband, and her body was now buried next to his at the burial ground near the church where they had served.

When Britt arrived at the church building, Pastor Joshudo was in his study. The pastor saw the expression on Britt's face and said, "You look upset, Chief Claiborne."

"I am, Pastor." Britt held up the envelope. "I received a letter today from Benjamin Harrison, the new United States president. I think you need to know what he had to say."

Joshudo gestured toward a nearby sofa. "Let us sit down."

After they had eased onto the sofa, Britt told Joshudo that the letter said the president and the U. S. Congress planned to mark off areas of land within Oklahoma District for the Indians to live on, and that those areas would be called "reservations."

Joshudo frowned. "Why would they do this?"

"Because President Harrison says that the United States government is going to allow white people to enter Oklahoma District and claim what will be known as 'unassigned lands.' White settlers may claim 160 acres of land per family, and those who live on and improve their claim for five years will then receive title to it."

Joshudo took a deep breath. "Chief Claiborne, this is very bad news. From what I had been taught in school as a boy, and from what I have read in recent history books, this move by President Harrison and Congress is very much like what happened to the Cherokees and the other four Civilized Tribes in this country a half-century ago. This land in what was called Indian Territory for such a long time is *our* land. And now we will be forced to give up most of it to the white people? This is bad. *Very* bad!"

"I agree, Pastor Joshudo. President Harrison also says in his letter that he will be sending troops to Oklahoma District to make sure the Indians move to and settle on the land assigned to them. He then will advise every newspaper in the country of the Unassigned Lands Bill and give them a date when the white settlers may come and look at the 160-acre plots. Then in a land rush a few days later, they may make their move to claim them."

Joshudo's jaw firmed, and fury touched his dark eyes. "Chief Claiborne, I am very angry at what is happening to our people! You and I both know that all the Indians in Oklahoma District will be angry, too. This is *our* land, and now the white man's government will give most of it to the white people. We must do something!"

Britt sighed and scrubbed a palm over his face. "I'm afraid there's nothing we can do, Pastor. The United States Army will see to it that the Indians make no trouble over this plan. Blood will be shed if we do. *Indian* blood."

Pastor Joshudo bit his lower lip, sighed, and said, "You are right, Chief. You were once an officer in the United States Army. You know what would happen if we tried to rise up against this decree. We have no choice but to obey. I...I know the Lord can give grace to us Christians, but I fear what those who are not Christians might do." The pastor laid a hand on Britt's arm. "Let us pray about this."

Together, the two heavy-hearted men knelt beside the sofa and prayed, earnestly asking for God's help.

That evening, Britt showed Cherokee Rose the letter he had received from President Harrison, then told her its contents.

"I don't understand this, Britt!" she said, indignation in her voice. "How can the government do this to us again? What right do they have to treat the Indians this way? You and I and a lot of other Indians here are too old to pick up and move elsewhere. And why should we have to? Why can't they leave us alone!"

Britt took hold of her shoulders and looked into her flaming eyes. "Sweetheart, I know it isn't right, but we both know that when white man's government speaks, we have no choice but to obey. To do otherwise would only bring grief and pain."

Cherokee Rose bit her lower lip.

"At least this time we won't have to make that long, tedious journey like we did before."

"I know, but according to these 'reservation' boundaries you just told me about, the Indians will be given the poorest land to live on."

"Yes, that's true, and I'm as upset about it as you are. But we can't stand and fight against the government and their military power. We have no artillery to launch a battle against them, and besides, we're greatly outnumbered. Somehow we must live in peace with the white people who will be rushing in here to claim the best of the land." Britt took a deep breath. "Sweetheart, we must remember that the Lord is in control of all this. And difficult as it will be, His grace is all-sufficient for us."

Cherokee Rose closed her eyes and nodded. "It is just so unfair. We have not been able to fully trust most of the United States presidents. We have seldom been able to believe what they were telling us."

"There's no doubt in my mind that when President Cleveland led Congress to change the name of our land from Indian Territory to Oklahoma District, he already had in mind to move white people in here and put us on reservations. The new president hasn't been in office long enough to come up with all of this on his own."

"I am trying to hold my temper in check, Britt, but I have to say that the Indians have been treated like second-class people ever since white men first stepped foot on what was our country. We were here first!"

"Yes, we were. But even though this new edict is unfair, the Lord can equal it out. Though we born-again Indians are in the minority here, we are God's children. We can trust Him to take care of us."

A smile erased the tightness that had been on Cherokee Rose's face. "You are so wise, my love. With your leadership as chief of police, our people will follow, and we will once again survive and be at peace."

Then she rose up on her tiptoes and kissed him soundly.

The next day, Police Chief Britt Claiborne sent mounted messengers to all the Indian chiefs of Oklahoma District, announcing that there would be an important meeting in three days at Tahlequah.

When that day arrived, all the chiefs of the Cherokee, the Chickasaw, the Choctaw, the Creek, and the Seminole tribes were in attendance. Britt stood before them, showed them the letter he had received from President Benjamin Harrison, and explained its contents.

Angry shouts came from the crowd, and some urged the others gathered there to resist this new edict, by force if necessary. But eventually all agreed with Britt Claiborne that if they and their people fought against President Harrison's decree, they would only suffer for it.

After the meeting was over, the Christian chiefs met with Britt and prayed together, asking the Lord to give them the grace, the strength, and the wisdom to lead their people as this plan was enacted in their homeland.

In the last week of January 1889, every newspaper in the United States—including the *Cherokee Phoenix*—carried the announcement from President Benjamin Harrison about the Unassigned Lands Bill, saying that prospective white settlers were welcome to appear at designated spots on the borders of Oklahoma District. United States Army units would be there to oversee them as they were allowed to enter the District at any time from March 2 through April 21 to look the land over and pick out the 160-acre parcels each family would like to own.

It was emphasized in bold print that they could not claim the parcels at that time, however. On April 22, the army units would oversee a land rush that would allow prospective settlers to dash onto the 2 million available acres to lay claim to their 160-acre sites. After April 22, prospective settlers could come and stake their claims under army supervision as long as land was available.

twenty-three

n Thursday, January 31, 1889, it was a cold day in Wichita, Kansas, with light snow falling from a low, gunmetal-gray sky.

In the Ackerman house on Kellogg Street, twenty-eight-year-old Martha Ackerman stood on the opposite side of the bed from the family doctor in the bedroom where her husband, Troy, lay while the doctor checked his vital signs. Dr. Russell Stockton had diagnosed twenty-nine-year-old Troy with consumption some fourteen months previously and checked on him an average of every two weeks.

Martha's parents, Will and Essie Baker, who were farmers in their early fifties, stood together a few feet from the bed. Close to their grandparents were Troy and Martha's three somber-faced children: eight-year-old Angie, six-year-old Eddie, and Elizabeth, who was four.

"Be honest with me, Dr. Stockton," Troy said weakly as the doctor began to put his stethoscope and other instruments into their leather bag. "How much time do I have left?"

The doctor closed his bag, ran a hesitant look to the Bakers and the Ackerman children, then to Martha. He took a deep breath and looked down at the ailing man. "I cannot lie to you, Troy. By every indication, I have to tell you that you don't have very long. Maybe a week. Two at the most. I'm sorry."

Angie, Eddie, and Elizabeth began crying and rushed to their mother. Martha folded them in her arms, weeping herself. Martha's parents came and embraced their daughter and grandchildren as they shed their own tears.

The doctor picked up his bag and patted Troy's shoulder. "I know you all want to be alone with Troy. I'll leave you some medicine for his pain, and if you need more, please let me know. Either way, I'll be back to see him on Monday."

"Thank you, Dr. Stockton, for all that you've done for Troy during these months of his illness," Martha said.

A mist formed in the doctor's eyes. His voice trembled as he said, "Martha, I am so sorry."

Martha palmed tears from her cheeks. "You needn't be sorry, Dr. Stockton. You did everything possible to save Troy's life."

After Martha walked the doctor to the front door of the house, she returned to the bedroom and paused in the doorway. Her children and her parents were standing together at the side of Troy's bed. Will was holding Essie's hand.

Sobbing, Angie cried, "Oh, Papa, I love you!"

Troy reached out and with a weak, shaky hand, patted the cheeks of all three of his children. "I love you so much, my precious babies."

Martha stepped up to her children and gathered them close around her. "You know," she said, "though Dr. Stockton says Papa's time with us is short, Jesus is the Great Physician. Our days on earth are actually in *His* hands."

Will and Essie were trying to smile as the children looked up at their mother.

Martha's eyes shimmered with tears as she looked down at her husband. His face was gray, his eyes dull and sunken. She thought back, recalling how vibrant and handsome he was before the consumption attacked his body.

Troy reached toward her, and Martha took his hand.

He licked his dry lips and made a faint smile. "Yes, our Lord Jesus is the Great Physician, and He can spare my life if He so desires. But just in case it's God's time to take me home, I want to make sure that my family is taken care of to the best of my ability."

"What do you mean, Troy?" Will said. "What can you possibly do?"

Troy looked up at his father-in-law. "Did you happen to read the article in yesterday's *Wichita Chronicle* about the upcoming land rush in Oklahoma District?"

"No. We seldom buy a newspaper."

"Well, the article took up the whole front page. Martha read it to me yesterday, and we talked about it at length. We were going to show it to you if you hadn't seen it." He looked at Martha. "Honey, would you go get the paper and read it to your parents, please?"

Martha returned shortly with the paper and read the article to them.

"Will and Essie," Troy said, "since you've given us almost all of your spare money to help pay for my medical bills, I want you take Martha and the children to Oklahoma District come spring and lay claim to one of those 160-acre sites. Your small farm here just isn't able to produce enough for all of you to live on."

Angie looked at her father through tears and cried, "Papa, we're not going to leave you!"

Troy took hold of her hand. "Sweetheart, I said Grandpa and Grandma should take you in the spring. You heard what Dr. Stockton said. At the most, I have two weeks to live. I...I can't explain it exactly, but I feel quite certain that it will soon be my time to go to heaven." He set his eyes on his father-in-law and had to take two short breaths before he could speak. "Will, you need to begin making plans right away."

Will nodded, but could not find his voice.

"I can rest easy if I know that my dear family will have a home where they can make a good living," Troy said, his voice growing weaker with each labored breath. "I know it will be a lot of hard work to pick up and move, but I've heard about the rich farmland in Oklahoma District. You'll do well there, I'm sure. I want so much for my precious wife and children and in-laws to have a new place to call home."

Martha bent over Troy, wiping tears from her cheeks, and gave him a radiant smile. "Darling, we will do as you have asked. You can rest easy now."

Troy was able to produce a smile. "Thank you. I don't want you ever to forget me, nor the beautiful life we've had together. But as you go on living, I want you to find happiness and fulfillment."

While Martha tried to maintain her composure, Troy ran his gaze over his family, coughed, sucked for air, and as he had done many times since becoming so ill, reminded them that as

Christians, they go to a far better place when they leave this world. He did not want them to mourn for him when he died. He would be in heaven with Jesus.

On Saturday, February 9, Troy Ackerman died while Dr. Russell Stockton was at his bedside, having been summoned for Martha by a neighbor because he was coughing violently and in a great deal of pain.

Troy was given a heart-touching funeral by the family's pastor.

On Sunday, February 17, after the morning church service, Martha, her children, and her parents went to the cemetery at the edge of town to pay a last visit to Troy's grave.

Early the next morning, they all left Wichita in the Baker wagon for Oklahoma District. It was a cold, clear day. As the heavily laden wagon left the outskirts of Wichita, Martha looked back toward the cemetery and said to Troy, *I'm sorry to leave your grave, but of course you are not there anyhow. You are in heaven. And one day we will be reunited in our bright, heavenly home.*

Dabbing with a handkerchief at the tears that surfaced in her eyes, she squared her shoulders and faced a new tomorrow.

On that same Monday in Amarillo, Texas, Lee Belden, who was in his late twenties, entered the Panhandle National Bank and made his way to the desk of bank president Michael Vandenburg's secretary.

Hattie Williams, who knew Lee and his wife well, smiled and said, "Good morning, Lee. I suppose you're here to see Mr. Vandenburg about the letter we mailed to you last Thursday."

Lee's face was grim. "Yes."

Hattie's mouth turned down. "I'm so sorry this is happening to you and Kathy."

"Yeah, me too. I'm here to ask Mr. Vandenburg to give us more time to turn things around."

Hattie nodded. "Please sit down, Lee. Mr. Vandenburg is with another customer at the moment. I'll get you in to see him when he's free."

Lee glanced at the closed door of the president's office and sat down in the nearby chair that Hattie had indicated.

The young farmer was staring at the floor when Hattie said, "Lee, just between you and me, I seriously doubt that you and Kathy are going to be shown any mercy."

He lifted his head and met her gaze. "You mean we're going to lose the farm?"

"Unless you can come up with the money to get current on your loan payments, that's what's going to happen, I'm afraid. Of course, I could be wrong. Maybe when you talk to him, you'll touch some nerve that I don't know he has."

"Slim chance, though, huh?"

"I think so. Have you heard about what's going on in Oklahoma District, though?"

"What do you mean?"

"The 160-acre land parcels that are going to be given away there to American citizens who join the land rush the government's sponsoring. I understand it's excellent farmland."

Lee shook his head. "I don't know anything about it."

Hattie pulled a newspaper from one of her desk drawers. "I learned about it from this January 30 edition of the *North Texas Daily News*. Knowing what the drought has done to some of the farmers like yourself who have mortgages here, I picked up several copies and have given them to those unfortunate people."

"I'd like to read it."

"I'll save this copy for you. If you still want it after you've talked to Mr. Vandenburg, it's yours."

"I appreciate that, Hattie."

At that moment, the door of the president's office came open, and a male customer with silver hair came out. As he made for the front door of the bank, Hattie said, "Mr. Vandenburg, Mr. Belden is here to see you."

Vandenburg's features tightened. "All right. Come on in, Lee."

After the two men entered the office and sat down, Vandenburg said, "I assume that you're here because of the letter about the bank making preparations to repossess your farm."

"Yes, sir. I'm here to ask you to have mercy on me, Mr. Vandenburg, and give me a chance to get back on my feet. You know how this drought has taken its toll on so many farms, including mine. It has made it impossible for my wife and me to keep up with the mortgage payments. The reason I've been able to make some of the payments is that I've done some carpentry work for people in Amarillo, but that work has come to a stop. I know I'm eight months behind on the payments, but I'm asking you to give me a chance to find some other kind of work. Please don't foreclose on our mortgage."

Michael Vandenburg rose to his feet. "This being behind on your mortgage payments has gone on too long already, Lee. Enough is enough. You and your family have exactly two weeks to vacate that property. It will be repossessed two weeks from today, March 4. Now, I must ask you to leave. I have work to do."

Feeling queasy, Lee hurried from Vandenburg's office, closed the door behind him, and moved up to Hattie Williams's desk.

She looked up and frowned. "It didn't go so good, Lee?"

"Not at all. I'll take that paper you offered."

Hattie smiled and handed the newspaper to him. "I'll be interested to know if you and Kathy decide to go to Oklahoma District."

"We'll keep you posted. Thanks for the paper."

When Lee Belden arrived home, Kathy and their two sons, nine-year-old Brent and six-year-old Brian, were at the front door to meet him.

"I can tell by the look on your face that you have bad news," Kathy said.

"Yeah. Vandenburg gave us two weeks from today to be out of the house and off the property. The bank is going to foreclose on us."

Kathy broke into tears, and Lee took her into his arms. The boys broke down and cried, seeing their mother weeping.

Lee held Kathy till her weeping began to subside, then he said, "Okay, now I want all three of you to dry your tears. Let's go into the parlor and sit down. I have some *good* news for you."

"You mean about what we're going to do since we've lost the farm?" Kathy said.

Lee nodded, and Kathy noted that his face no longer showed anger and disappointment, but rather was shining.

"What have you got up your sleeve, Lee Belden?"

"Something exciting, honey. Let's go sit down, and I'll tell you all about it."

When they were all seated, Lee opened the newspaper he had been carrying and showed them the headlines, then read the article about the upcoming land rush in Oklahoma District.

Kathy felt excitement building in her heart.

Brent's eyes were wide. "Wow, Papa, that sounds good to me!"

Lee smiled. "I stopped at the newspaper office before leaving town and asked them if they had any information on how the weather has been in Oklahoma District. They get a weather report by telegraph every day for the whole country. They showed me in their records what Oklahoma District's weather has been since last July. There was lots of rain up until late October, then lots of snow ever since. There's plenty of water…no drought."

Lee and Kathy discussed it thoroughly, and soon they agreed that they should go to Oklahoma District and establish their new home on one of the 160-acre farms. If they left soon, they would be there in time to begin looking the land over by March 2. They would live in the family wagon until they could lay claim to a good section of farmland on April 22, and get a house built.

The next day, the Beldens packed their meager belongings into the large wagon and drove off the farm. They stopped in Amarillo long enough to let Hattie Williams know what they were doing, then drove east out of town and headed for Oklahoma District.

In late February 1889, Gloria Parker, who then lived in a small rented shack in Joplin, Missouri, was writing a letter to her husband, Craig, who had been an inmate at the Missouri State Prison at Jefferson City for over four years. Because it was over two hundred miles from Joplin to Jefferson City, Gloria could visit her husband only about once every two months.

Just as Gloria closed off the letter, there was a knock at the front door.

She laid the pen down and hurried to the door. When she

opened it, she was surprised to see a man with a badge on his chest standing there.

"Good morning, ma'am," the husky middle-aged man said, touching his hat brim. "You *are* Mrs. Parker, correct?"

"Yes, sir."

"I'm Deputy U.S. Marshal Jack Waltham, Mrs. Parker. I work out of the office in Jefferson City. I have some very good news for you. May I come in?"

"Of course, deputy. We can sit down in the parlor."

When they sat down in the tiny parlor, facing each other, Gloria asked, "What is this good news?"

"Your husband is going to be released from prison, ma'am."

Gloria's eyes widened. "Wha—? H-how has this happened?"

"Well, I'm here to tell you the story."

"Would you like a cup of coffee first?" she said, her heart pounding in her chest. "It's hot on the stove in the kitchen."

"That sounds good."

Gloria hurried to the small kitchen and returned with two steaming cups.

"Mrs. Parker, I've read the whole story about your husband's arrest for bank robbery in July 1885 and his claim of innocence," Waltham said. "Well, ma'am, the man who actually committed the robbery was just caught robbing a bank in Columbia."

Gloria looked toward heaven and said, "Oh, thank You, Lord Jesus! You knew Craig had not robbed that bank. Thank You for letting the truth come out."

Jack Waltham smiled and said, "I take it you're a born-again child of God, Mrs. Parker."

Happy tears glistened in Gloria's eyes. "I am! And you must be, too?"

"Yes, ma'am. I received the Lord Jesus as my Saviour when I

was a teenager. Is your husband a Christian?"

Gloria's mouth turned down. "No, he isn't. I was saved at a revival meeting just before Craig went to prison. I've tried to give the gospel to him every time I've visited him at the prison, but he won't listen. I've been praying all this time that the Lord would bring about circumstances in Craig's life that would draw him to Jesus. And since God has now seen fit to let the guilty bank robber be caught, I'm encouraged to believe that He'll also draw Craig to Himself."

"I've watched the Lord work in wonderful ways to bring lost souls to salvation in answer to prayer, ma'am. I have no doubt that it's going to happen in this case, too."

"Yes! Yes, I just know Craig is going to get saved!" Gloria said as the tears streamed down her cheeks.

twenty-four

loria Parker wiped the tears from her face and said to Deputy U.S. Marshal Jack Waltham, "I would like to know the details about the real bank robber getting caught, and I'd like to know his name."

"The man's name is Hector Jamison," Waltham said. "He was shot by a bank officer while robbing the Columbia State Bank yesterday morning. As he lay on the floor of the bank's lobby, Jamison knew he was dying, and he told the town marshal that he, not Craig Parker, had actually robbed the Joplin

National Bank. He was sorry that Craig had gone to prison for a crime he didn't commit, and Jamison said he didn't want to die with this on his conscience. He died a few minutes after his confession."

Gloria let out a sigh. "We lost our farm just outside of Joplin shortly after Craig was sent to prison. There was no way I could keep up the mortgage payments. Now, at least, we can start over and have our own home. How soon will they release Craig from prison?"

Waltham smiled. "As soon as you and I get there."

"You mean…I'm going with you so I can be there when they let him out?"

"Exactly. You see, ma'am, your husband hasn't yet been told that he's going to be released. He doesn't know about Hector Jamison or his confession. Warden Duane Dahlman thought you might like to be there when Craig is told the story."

"Oh, wonderful! I've met Warden Dahlman. He was very nice to me." Gloria clapped her hands together. "I sure *do* want to be there when Craig is told that he's being set free!"

"Mrs. Parker, when were you there to visit your husband last?" Waltham asked as Gloria thumbed tears from her eyes.

"Just last week."

"How often do you usually visit him?"

"About every two months. That's all I can afford."

The deputy chuckled. "Then won't he be surprised to see you today!"

At eleven o'clock that morning, Gloria Parker was on the train headed for Jefferson City, sitting beside Deputy U.S. Marshal Jack Waltham.

At the same time, in the Missouri State Prison just outside Jefferson City, Craig Parker was standing in his cell looking down at his cell mate, Willie Dalton, who lay dead on the floor. Three guards were there, along with the prison physician, Dr. James Bell, and the prison chaplain, Curtis Robins.

Willie had been having chest pains for several days. Only moments before, he had grasped his chest while sitting on the bunk, extreme pain showing on his twisted features. Craig had called for a guard, who sent for Dr. Bell, but Willie was dead before the doctor could get to the cell.

As two of the guards were carrying the body away with the doctor beside them, Craig said to the other guard and the chaplain, "It could've been me. I'm only thirty-one, but Willie was two years younger than me."

The guard nodded and met Craig's gaze. "It can happen to anybody. Well, Chaplain, we'd better get going."

"I want to stay with Craig for a while," Chaplain Robins said. "You go on."

When the guard was gone, Craig turned to Robins with tears in his eyes. "Chaplain, you led Willie to the Lord three months ago." His forehead was damp with perspiration, and he was squeezing his hands together until the knuckles were shiny white. "Willie's now in heaven, right?"

"He sure is."

"If it had been me who died, I'd be in hell right now. Chaplain, I can't stand it any longer. I want to be saved!"

Chaplain Robins sat down on Craig's bunk beside him and opened his Bible. He went over the plan of salvation with Craig as he had done many times before. Within a few minutes, he was able to lead Craig Parker to the Lord.

With tears of joy spilling down his face, Craig gripped the

chaplain's hand and said, "Thank you for not giving up on me, Chaplain Robins. Oh, how happy Gloria's going to be when I write her and tell her that I've been born again!"

It was almost three o'clock that afternoon, and Craig, alone in his cell, had just finished writing the letter to tell Gloria that her prayers had been answered.

A guard stepped up to the barred door. "Parker, the warden wants to see you in his office."

Craig laid the pencil and paper down on his bunk and stood up. "What's he want to see me about?"

The guard inserted the key in the lock and turned it. "You'll soon find out."

As the guard ushered Craig down the corridor toward Warden Dahlman's office, Craig tried to get him to tell him what was going on, but the guard would say no more.

They soon reached the warden's office door, and when the guard opened it and Craig stepped into the office, he was startled to see Gloria there. She stood up and headed toward him as the guard stepped back into the corridor and closed the door. The warden looked on from behind his desk.

"Honey, you were just here a few days ago," Craig said, taking hold of Gloria's hands. "Is something wrong?"

Gloria smiled. "Nothing is wrong, darling. Something is very *right*."

Craig glanced at the warden, who was now on his feet, smiling, then looked at Gloria. A brilliant smile broke over his own face. "Before you tell me about this something that's very right, let me tell you something about me, personally, that's now very right."

"All right. I'd like to know what has put that radiant smile on your face."

Craig pulled her closer to him and felt tears form in his eyes. "Your prayers have been answered, sweetheart. Chaplain Robins led me to the Lord this morning!"

Gloria's eyes widened and glistened with tears as she cried, "Oh, Craig, am I dreaming?"

He folded her in his arms and kissed her cheek. "No, you're wide awake. Your husband is now a born-again man!"

The warden looked on, fighting his own tears as the happy couple clung to each other, their hearts overflowing with joy. Craig told Gloria what a fool he had been to resist the gospel all his life and that he was sure the Lord had let him be convicted for a crime he didn't commit so He could get his attention. He told her about Willie Dalton, a Christian who died that very morning, which caused Craig to finally tell Chaplain Robins that he wanted to be saved.

"Oh, Craig, I'm so glad for you!" Gloria said, hugging him tight. "I've prayed so hard."

"I know you have, and I can never thank you enough for not giving up on this stubborn sinner."

The warden was now beside them and said, "As a Christian myself, Parker, I'm thrilled to hear this. Now, I want you two to come and sit down. I'm going to explain what your dear wife meant when she told you something was 'very right.'"

After Craig had been told the story of Hector Jamison's confession, the warden then told him he was a free man. Craig and Gloria shed tears of joy, and the warden allowed them some time alone in a small office next to his.

"Honey, I don't want us to stay in Joplin," Craig said after the happy couple had clung to each other for several minutes. "Even though I've now been cleared of the crime, if we stay in Joplin, I'll still live under the stigma of having been in prison. We need to find a new place to call home."

Gloria smiled, her eyes sparkling with anticipation. "I whole-heartedly agree, sweetheart. Joplin holds nothing for us now. We can go wherever we want to. A fresh start sounds wonderful to me."

"Good!" Craig said. Then he brought up the land rush story from the newspapers he had been reading in the prison and told her he wanted to go to Oklahoma District, pick out 160 acres of good farmland, and start a new life.

"Of course, we'll have to build a house, barn, and outbuild-ings, and begin farming all over again, but with the Lord's help, we can do it."

Gloria's eyes were sparkling. "It sounds perfect to me. Neither of us is afraid of hard work, and a place of our own sounds won-derful!"

On the night train ride to Joplin, Craig Parker told his wife that while he was in prison, he checked a book out of the library that told the story of the North Carolina Cherokees' Trail of Tears and how well they did in settling and farming the land in Indian Territory.

He went on to tell Gloria how the beloved Cherokee Chief Sequoyah—who had given the Cherokee people their own alpha-bet and had translated the Bible into the Cherokee language—had written a message on a piece of paper the night of his death, alone and aware that he was dying: "The stars are bright tonight."

"The book explained that this was Chief Sequoyah's way of letting his people know how happy he was that though they had been forced out of their ancestral homes, they had found a new place to call home and were happy there."

Gloria nodded and smiled. "Bless his heart."

"So when Chief Sequoyah wrote, 'The stars are bright tonight,' it was his way of letting his people know that he died happy." Craig put his arm around his wife, glanced through the coach window at the stars, looked back at her, and said, "Yes, my sweetheart, the stars *are* bright tonight!"

epilogue

he venerable Chief Sequoyah was so admired by United States government leaders that, in his memory, the giant redwood trees of California's Pacific Coast and the Sierra Nevada were named after him. Some time before his death, newspapers began spelling his name *Sequoia*, thus the giant redwoods are called *Sequoia sempervirens*. California's 386,000-acre Sequoia National Park was also named after him.

Travel along the Trail of Tears
A Place to Call Home series

By Al & JoAnna Lacy

Cherokee Rose—Book One
Cherokee Rose, an eighteen-year-old
Indian girl, falls for Lieutenant Britt
Claiborne along the Trail of Tears.
If dreams come true, they'll one day
marry and find a place to call home
together.
Available Now!

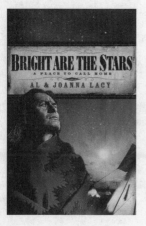

Bright Are the Stars—Book Two
Britt Claiborne and Cherokee Rose
settle into married life as the North
Carolina Cherokees settle into their new
home in Indian Territory. Hope-filled
beginnings thrive under the twinkling
heavens above.
Available Now!

The Land of Promise—Book Three
Available February 2007!

GOLD GLIMMERS, AND THE RUSH IS ON!

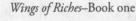

NEW DREAMS OF GOLD TRILOGY
By Al & JoAnna Lacy

Wings of Riches–Book one
Get in on the first book in a new trilogy by master narrators Al and JoAnna Lacy. Set in North America's nineteenth-century gold country, the tales are adventure filled and gripping!
ISBN 1-59052-389-X

The Forbidden Hills–Book Two
Jim Bannon leaves his family's Wyoming farm in hot pursuit of gold in the Black Hills of Dakota Territory. Will he secure the wealth that is his ticket to marry the love of his life?
ISBN 1-59052-477-2

The Golden Stairs–Book Three
Livia does not expect to meet anyone like Matt Holden on the Golden Stairs. While he saves her life, no one knows if her father has been as fortunate...
ISBN 1-59052-561-2

Frontier Doctor Trilogy

One More Sunrise–Book One
Young frontier doctor Dane Logan is gaining renown as a surgeon. Beyond his wildest hopes, he meets his long-lost love—only to risk losing her to the Tag Moran gang.
ISBN 1-59052-308-3

Beloved Physician–Book Two
While Dr. Dane gains renown by rescuing people from gunfights, Indian attacks, and a mine collapse, Nurse Tharyn mourns the capture of her dear friend Melinda by renegade Utes.
ISBN 1-59052-313-X

The Heart Remembers–Book Three
In this final book in the Frontier Doctor trilogy, Dane survives an accident, but not without losing his memory. Who is he? Does he have a family somewhere?
ISBN 1-59052-351-2

Hannah of Fort Bridger Series

Hannah Cooper's husband dies on the dusty Oregon Trail, leaving her in charge of five children and a general store in Fort Bridger. Dependence on God fortifies her against grueling challenges and bitter tragedies.

Angel of Mercy Series

Post-Civil War nurse Breanna Baylor uses her professional skill to bring healing to the body, and her faith in the Redeemer to bring comfort to thirsty souls, valiantly serving God on the dangerous frontier.

Shadow of Liberty Series

Let Freedom Ring
#1 in the Shadow of Liberty Series
It is January 1886 in Russia. Vladimir Petrovna, a Christian husband and father of three, faces bankruptcy, persecution for his beliefs, and despair. The solutions lie across a perilous sea.
ISBN 1-57673-756-X

The Secret Place
#2 in the Shadow of Liberty Series
Popular authors Al and JoAnna Lacy offer a compelling question: As two young people cope with love's longings on opposite shores, can they find the serenity of God's covering in The Secret Place?
ISBN 1-57673-800-0

A Prince Among Them
#3 in the Shadow of Liberty Series
A bitter enemy of Queen Victoria kidnaps her favorite great-grandson. Emigrants Jeremy and Cecelia Barlow book passage on the same ship to America, facing a complex dilemma that only all-knowing God can set right.
ISBN 1-57673-880-9

Undying Love
#4 in the Shadow of Liberty Series
Nineteen-year-old Stephan Varda flees his own guilt and his father's rage in Hungary, finding undying love from his heavenly Father—and a beautiful girl—across the ocean in America.
ISBN 1-57673-930-9

The Orphan Train Trilogy

The Little Sparrows, Book #1
Kearney, Cheyenne, Rawlins. Reno, Sacramento, San Francisco. At each train station, a few lucky orphans from the crowded streets of New York City receive the fulfillment of their dreams: a home and family. This orphan train is the vision of Charles Loring Brace, founder of the Children's Aid Society, who cannot bear to see innocent children abandoned in the overpopulated cities of the mid–nineteenth century. Yet it is not just the orphans whose lives need mending—follow the train along and watch God's hand restore love and laughter to the right family at the right time!
ISBN 1-59052-063-7

All My Tomorows, Book #2
When sixty-two orphans and abandoned children leave New York City on a train headed out West, they have no idea what to expect. Will they get separated from their friends and siblings? Will their new families love them? Will a family even pick them at all? Future events are wilder than any of them could imagine—ranging from kidnappings and whippings to stowing away on wagon trains, from starting orphanages of their own to serving as missionaries to the Apache. No matter what, their paths are being watched by Someone who cares about and carefully plans all their tomorrows.
ISBN 1-59052-130-7

Whispers in the Wind, Book #3
Young Dane Weston's dream is to become a doctor. But it will take more than just determination to realize his goal, once his family is murdered and he ends up in a colony of street waifs begging for food. Then he ends up being mistaken for a murderer himself and sentenced to life in prison. Now what will become of his friendship with the pretty orphan girl Tharyn, who wanted to enter the medical profession herself? Does she feel he is anything more than a big brother to her? And will she ever write him again?
ISBN 1-59052-169-2